Simply
Irresistible

A NOVELIZATION BY

L. K. Wright

FROM A STORY BY

Judith Roberts

Dell

Published by
Dell Publishing
a division of
Random House, Inc.
1540 Broadway
New York, New York 10036

Visit us on the Web! www.randomhouse.com
Educators and librarians, for a variety of teaching tools, visit us at
www.randomhouse.com/teachers

ISBN: 0-440-22848-4
Printed in the United States of America
March 1999
10 9 8 7 6 5 4 3 2 1
OPM

One

It was just another Tuesday morning, and Amanda Shelton was standing on the walkway in the middle of the Brooklyn Bridge, looking at New York City shining in the early-morning light. The cobalt sky was still dotted with fading stars, and Manhattan's skyscrapers glistened like the Emerald City, a place where anything was possible.

Amanda liked standing on the great bridge and often walked the long boardwalk to her favorite spot between the big gray towers that held the suspension cables. There she would gaze at the city and dream. . . . She'd dream about falling in love, and she'd dream about becoming a great chef as her mother had been. And then Amanda would toss a coin in the river and make a wish. This morning, she dreamt of becoming even a *good* chef—and *soon*, because if she didn't, the way things were going her family's restaurant would have to close.

As she opened her hand, the sun sparkled on the silver dollar in her palm. The wind came up suddenly and blew through her long, wild locks. She tossed the coin—but instead of dropping into the river, it hovered in midair for a moment, somehow seeming to defy gravity. Seconds later, the wind picked up and the coin fell, making an imperceptible splash in the rushing water below. *That's odd*, Amanda thought. Maybe it wasn't just another ordinary Tuesday, after all. . . .

Full of anticipation, she walked off the bridge and into the city, up Broadway to the Union Square market, where farmers from all over sold their wares. A jumble of tarp-covered stalls lined Union Square Park, their tables overflowing with peppers and cucumbers; peaches, plums, and nectarines; lobsters from Long Island; and goat cheese from upstate. Amanda loved the market and the people there, the vendors and the shoppers, the smells of herbs and fresh produce in the morning air. She had been coming to the market since she was born; her mother had always shopped there for the best produce for their restaurant. The vendors had become

Amanda's family, especially after her mother had died the year before and Amanda had come home from college early to keep the restaurant going.

Amanda walked into the canopied market just as a red apple came hurtling toward her. Her hand darted up like a professional catcher's and the apple smacked into her palm. She took a bite and smiled. "Delicious!" she yelled across the stalls.

"No—McIntosh!" Mr. Verini, the apple farmer, laughed. "Want some?"

"No, thanks. I'd better stick to the usual," Amanda answered. "Who knows what would happen if I didn't? I'd probably end up with applesauce instead of apple pie."

"Have a little faith in yourself," Mr. Verini said, handing her the bag of apples.

"Thanks," Amanda said. "See you Thursday, Mr. Verini."

"Come rain or shine," he said, smiling.

Amanda made her way to the mushroom stall, where Abe and his nephew, Charlie, were helping a customer. Amanda was surprised to see

Charlie. She had known him since they were both kids, running under the tables and through the stalls together. He was cute and very sweet, and he seemed to like her, but . . . she just didn't get goose bumps, the way she thought she should about a guy.

"Welcome back," she said. "School's out already?"

"Last week. Abe here put me right to work," Charlie said. "You think you'll go back and finish, now that your place is closing?"

"What do you mean *closing*?"

Abe kicked Charlie under the table.

"Hey, stop kicking me, Abe," Charlie cried.

"We're *not* closing," Amanda insisted, fear catching in her throat.

"He's confused," Abe said, knocking Charlie's head. Charlie quickly changed the subject. "Laurie Robinson's having a party Saturday. You want to come with me?" he asked.

Amanda searched through the many wild mushrooms, avoiding Charlie's eyes and worrying over what he had said about the restaurant. Could Abe and Charlie know something she didn't? "I'm sorry, but I've got to work," she answered at last. "But thanks anyway. Abe, where are my portobellos?"

"They're gone," he said sheepishly. "Valderon wanted them."

"Gone?"

"It was *Valderon* . . . you understand," Abe said, staring across the market in awe at Michel Valderon, the world-famous chef from Paris. Amanda followed his gaze and saw a man waving his arms and shouting in French, surrounded by several worried-looking younger men. They were buying up everything in sight. Next to Valderon stood a handsome young man in a tailored suit who looked more impatient than worried. Amanda couldn't take her eyes off him.

"At least you spotted him," a voice said.

Amanda turned to see an old vendor sitting between two stalls, a basket of crabs at his feet. He smiled at her, his face full of mischief.

"I've never even heard of him," Amanda said.

"Not Valderon. The other one," the old man said, nodding at the handsome man and winking.

Amanda felt embarrassed. "I don't remember

seeing you before. Are you always here?" she asked.

"Only when necessary," he said. "It's a very long trip." He smiled enigmatically and offered her the basket of crabs. "These are yours. Peeky toes. Marvelous," he said.

"Oh, no. . . . I wouldn't know what to do with a crab," she said.

"Sometimes desperate times require desperate measures. You'll be surprised by what you can learn," the old vendor said. He held out the basket.

Amanda laughed. "That's a good one," she said, slightly confused. Who *was* this guy? "Thanks anyway." And she walked away.

The old man called after her, "It's always important to remember: The wind from one door closing, opens another."

Amanda kept walking, chuckling at the odd little man. "Okay, fine. Whatever . . ." She walked over to the berry vendors, her friend T. J. Russo and T.J.'s young daughter, Molly. Amanda bought some raspberries for the tart she wanted to bake and headed toward a vegetable stand.

The little man with the basket of crabs appeared again.

"Weren't you just over *there*?" Amanda asked.

"Take my crabs, Amanda," he said. "Your mother wants you to start living up to your potential."

"My mother's dead."

"That's no reason to ignore her."

"Did you know her?" Amanda asked, suspicious.

Suddenly Valderon swept down on them and grabbed the basket of crabs. "Peeky toes!" he cried. "I must have them! *Maintenant!*"

"Hey, you can't take everything!" Amanda cried.

Valderon turned to the old man. "*Monsieur . . . vraiment.* I will pay double," he said, and then he smiled condescendingly at Amanda. "*S'il vous plaît, mademoiselle.*"

The little man locked Valderon in his gaze. "*Un homme qui a cuit son chat pour verifier une recette ne merite pas mes crabes!*"

Valderon seemed horrified by what the man

had told him. He dropped the basket and ran away, completely spooked. Amanda, who had learned French in school, had understood everything and was a little spooked herself.

"He really did that?" she asked. "He cooked his own cat to test a recipe?"

The old vendor nodded.

"That's disgusting!" she exclaimed.

"Any man who does that does not deserve my crabs," the old man said. Amanda watched one of the worried-looking men arguing with Valderon.

"So that's what happened to my little Chouchou! You said she ran away!" the man yelled at Valderon.

"*Tais-toi!* Shut up!" Valderon yelled back.

Amanda glanced around for the great-looking guy who had been with Valderon, but he seemed to have left. She felt disappointed. Just then a crab jumped out of the basket and grabbed the hem of her skirt.

"I guess they really are mine," she laughed, brushing it off.

"Fifty-nine dollars, please," the crab man said,

watching the crab scuttle down the path. "Don't let him get away."

Amanda handed the man three twenty-dollar bills and took off after the runaway crab. It crab-walked down the crowded pavement, dodging the feet of shoppers, until it disappeared under the cloth hanging over a vegetable vendor's table. Amanda, on hands and knees, crawled after it.

The crab was cornered.

"Gotcha!" she laughed, but as she reached for the crab, it darted out from under the table. Amanda grabbed for the feisty little crustacean. She got hold of something and held on. When she crawled out from under the table, she discovered that the something was—a man's leg. Blushing, Amanda looked up to see it was *him*, the cute guy in the suit who'd been with Valderon. She was mortified. "Oh, no. . . . Hello. Excuse me, but I think something just went up your pants."

Amanda removed her hand from the man's pants leg and stood. "You probably think I'm some kind of weirdo." He looked at her, slightly bemused, his eyes shining. "But I'm not. I'm just trying to help you—"

"Ahhhhhh!" He jumped, shaking his leg—the crab had bitten him. It leapt from his pants leg and Amanda caught it neatly, trying not to laugh. The man stared at it, surprised and slightly embarrassed.

"I'm sorry, I tried to warn you," she said.

"Where'd that come from?" he asked. "How'd it get—?"

Amanda held the crab in her hands. "This one was determined to get away."

"Frisky little bugger."

"Not for long," Amanda said slyly. "I guess they're gonna be lunch at my restaurant. I'm preparing something . . . um . . . something very . . ." She panicked. She didn't have a clue what she was preparing. She'd never cooked a crab in her life—why was she boasting? Just then a bus went by with an advertisement for Napoleon Cognac on its side. "Something Napoleonic!" she exclaimed. "I mean, crab napoleon! With . . . spring tomatoes and . . . *pommes soufflées.* And truffled *haricots verts.* It should be very . . . insouciant!" She beamed, pleased with herself—and then suddenly, horribly self-conscious. *What was she saying?*

"I'm sure it will be." The man smiled at her. Goose bumps went up her sides, and she noticed his beautiful suit and tie, his good shoes and nice haircut. All at once she felt very disheveled and terribly shy. He was an uptown boy, that was clear. He probably only went out with uptown girls, like young executives and models. He was looking at her as if he'd never seen anyone like her before—was that good?

"You don't look like you're in the restaurant business," she said nervously.

"I don't? Why not?"

"The suit. Are you?"

"No," he said. He felt a bit confused. These early mornings with Valderon were a killer. And this girl, she was so, so—special. He'd never seen anyone so beautiful. "I mean yes. Yes, I'm opening a restaurant. And that maniac over there's the chef," he said, nodding toward Valderon, who was waving him over angrily. "And it looks like I'd better go. Nice meeting you. And your crab."

Amanda watched him walk away, wishing she had been able to keep him a little longer. She didn't even know his name. He probably had some snooty uptown girlfriend anyway, she thought with a sigh. She turned to head home. As she did, she bumped into the little old man holding the basket of crabs.

She laughed. "How do you move around so fast? You must know how to fly!"

The old man held out the basket and Amanda took it, wondering what in the world had possessed her to buy the crabs.

The man peered deeply into her eyes. "Your mother had some beautiful diamond earrings. You should wear them," he said with a grin. "They're the perfect spark to light the fire."

"I guess you knew her pretty well," Amanda said. "What's your name?"

"Gene O'Reilly. Nice to meet you."

Gene O'Reilly shook Amanda's hand, and then she walked away, absolutely befuddled by this strange man.

"Your change!" he yelled after her. She turned around and he flipped her a coin, which she caught easily. When she opened her palm, she was amazed to see it was the very same silver dollar she'd tossed into the river earlier that morning. When she looked up again, the old man had vanished.

Two

Amanda's aunt Stella sat at the upright piano in the empty restaurant and played a soft tune.

The Southern Cross Restaurant stood on a tree-lined street in downtown New York. It had the look of a place that had been there for decades but that you might walk by and never actually notice. It had been there a long time— eighty years was more than a lifetime for a restaurant in Manhattan, and it had been eighty years earlier when Amanda's grandfather had first opened the mahogany doors for business. Amanda's mother, Rose, had grown up in the kitchen, and so had Rose's older sister, Stella. When the girls were old enough, Rose had taken over the kitchen. Stella had taken over the dining room, greeting and seating customers, mixing drinks, serving food, and sometimes playing the old piano and singing. Stella's voice was as magical as Rose's cooking, and for a long time, the Southern Cross was a happy local hangout.

But times had changed. The people in the neighborhood were wealthier now and went to newer, trendier restaurants than the Southern Cross. And then Amanda's mother had died and it had been Amanda's turn in the kitchen. As much as she wanted to be a great chef, Amanda couldn't capture the magic her mother had, and slowly the restaurant's business had dried up. They couldn't afford to hire a chef, and Stella didn't have the heart to even suggest it, knowing how badly her niece wanted to be a great chef and keep the family business going. But time and their savings had run out, and as Stella picked out a tune on the old piano, she worried about how she could break the news to Amanda: After eighty years, the Southern Cross was going to have to close.

The bells on the front door jingled and Stella looked up to see Amanda coming in, a basket in her hands.

"There's some coffee for you on the bar,"

Stella said, still playing the piano. "What's in the basket?"

"Peeky toes," Amanda said. "I had the weirdest morning. First this guy made me buy these—he said he knew Mom. Gene O'Reilly. Do you know him?"

"I don't think so. Did he have red hair and a big nose?" Stella asked.

"No."

"Curly black hair and a crooked nose?"

"No. I think he was a crazy person, the way he was talking," Amanda mused. "But then Charlie—"

"Abe's nephew?"

"Yeah. He said we were closing. Why would he say that?"

Stella's fingers tangled on the piano keys, making a terrible sound. She gulped and closed the lid. How had they heard? She'd never meant for Amanda to find out that way.

Amanda eyed her aunt suspiciously as Stella started taking the chairs off the tables and setting up the restaurant for lunch.

Stella stalled. "So Charlie's back already? Did he ask you out?"

"Yes, he did, and no, I'm not going, and yes, my—"

"—expectations are too high," they said in unison.

They'd had this discussion many times before—too many, as far as Amanda was concerned. Amanda's aunt was a strapping blond woman of sixty who had never married—but not for lack of chances. Stella liked two things equally: She liked men, and she liked being free. She couldn't understand what was wrong with her young niece and was always encouraging her to go out on dates. But Amanda wanted to Fall In Love, not just go out to nightclubs and parties. She wanted to feel excited, she wanted to be swept off her feet by someone.

"If you're waiting for a prince, you're in the wrong country," her aunt continued. "Charlie's a perfectly good date. You could go dancing, or to the movies."

"Don't change the subject."

"What subject?" Stella said too innocently.

"The restaurant closing. I figured Charlie's wrong. I mean, we're running the place together, so

I would know something like that . . . wouldn't I, Aunt Stella?" Amanda asked pointedly.

Stella took a chair off a table and sat in it. She gestured for Amanda to do the same. "Amanda, sweetie, I've been meaning to talk to you about this, but, well, it never seemed like the right time to talk about something like this, given the nature of what it is that I need to talk to you about; it always seemed like exactly not the right time, so it didn't come up, and—"

Amanda interrupted her aunt's stammering and stalling. "I think this might be the right time," she said sternly.

Stella blurted it out: "The new landlord raised the rent and . . . we're not making it, Amanda. We haven't for months."

"How much did they raise the rent?"

"To five grand a month."

Amanda slammed a hand down on the table. "They can't do that. We'll fight it. There must be laws. We'll go to a bank, get a loan—"

"I *tried*," Stella said. "The way things have been going lately, the bank doesn't have faith we'd be able to pay it back."

"We've been here for eighty years," Amanda said. "It's *me* they don't have faith in." Tears filled her eyes.

Stella put her arms around her niece.

"I'm so sorry," Amanda cried. "This has been your whole life, and I just destroyed it—"

"Don't worry about me," Stella said soothingly. "I'll go to . . . Sardinia! Meet some nice, tall . . . Sardinian. Or maybe Thailand. I've never been to the East," she continued with false cheer. She was sad that the old place was going to close, but she didn't want Amanda feeling bad about it. Amanda was a young woman with her life ahead of her; Amanda could do anything, Stella believed, if she just wanted to badly enough.

Amanda got up and walked across the cozy room full of tables covered with blue-checked cloths. She stood at the bar her grandfather had built so long ago. "I used to tap dance on this bar, do you remember?" she said, running her hands along the smooth, polished wood.

"It's just a bar, honey," Stella said.

"It's not, though. This is all I ever wanted—to

run this place. To be a great chef, here, where I grew up. I can't believe this is it. I never even *thought* of doing anything else. If we had a few more months, I could try some simpler recipes—"

"I'm sorry, but it's too late. We can't afford next month's rent." Stella put her arm around Amanda and led her toward the kitchen. "Come on. You know what they say: The wind from one door slamming, opens another."

"What did you say?" Amanda was startled. Wasn't that what the man in the market had said? Amanda couldn't believe it was just a coincidence. But what else could it be?

"Did I get it wrong?" Stella asked. "I never can do proverbs. Come on, I'm starved. Make me something delicious," and they walked into the little kitchen together.

CHAPTER

Three

Tom Bartlett, the handsome man bitten by the crab in the market, stood before the crowd of reporters. "And after an exquisite meal at Jonathan's, our guests will have the run of the store. It's an entirely new approach to fine dining—and shopping. You'll see for yourselves next week. Thanks for coming," he said with a smile. He hoped he looked calm and cool, because he sure didn't feel that way.

A reporter called after him, "Fine restaurants in department stores have never worked before. And you've reportedly spent four million dollars on this one. That's a heavy gamble, isn't it?"

He couldn't let them rattle him. He had to pretend he was absolutely confident, even though secretly he was a nervous wreck. "Not when you have the right ingredients," he replied. He walked away from the video cameras and reporters huddled near the main entrance of the store and made his way through the cosmetics department. He nodded hello and greeted the staff. Tom loved his job as the head of the department store, and the staff seemed to love him, even if at twenty-eight he was younger than many of them.

The press conference had gone well, but all that mattered to Tom now was that the restaurant be a success. Jonathan's had been his idea, and his boss, Jonathan Bendel, was still skeptical. Tom had done everything he could to make sure it would be a wonderful place, from hiring the French master chef Valderon to choosing the most elegant china and glassware from around the world. Still, he was anxious. If opening night didn't go perfectly, Jonathan's could be the biggest financial disaster Bendel's department store had ever seen.

"Morning, Tom," Lois McNally said, grabbing his elbow and walking with him. Lois was the fashion director of Bendel's, and Tom's closest friend. She dressed in the latest fashions, wore her long strawberry blond hair loose, and had a sharp wit that kept Tom on his toes.

"There's a very thin girl in your office making herself at home," she said wickedly. Lois knew how skittish Tom was about girls getting too close to him too soon.

"Oh, no. It's Kris," Tom cried, horrified. "Why is she in my office without me?"

"I thought you'd want to know," Lois muttered.

They hurried up the sweeping central staircase to the executive suites.

Tom's office was as elegant and imposing as the store itself, with beautiful leather chairs, a huge desk, and a wall-sized computer screen.

Kris was sitting at Tom's desk, her laptop computer hooked into his. On the wall screen was Tom's monthly calendar, now full of flashing red entries. "I had a few minutes before my facial so I'm downloading my schedule onto yours," said Kris, a thin girl in black. "The red ones are the things I added. Just a few parties, dinners, some charity balls we're invited to. This way you won't miss a thing, and I'll always know where you are." She smiled.

"Great, great," Tom said weakly.

Kris picked up one of the many elaborate paper airplanes that sat on a stand behind Tom's desk. "*Tommy,* these are adorable," she teased.

Tom snatched it from her, gazing intensely at the paper model. "In 1961 Howard Hughes flew a paper airplane in Las Vegas from the Golden Nugget to the Sands Hotel—4.2 *miles.* I'm going to break that record when I unlock the secret of the adjustable sweepback. Which is in one of these."

Lois asked, "Wasn't Howard Hughes the guy who never got out of his PJs?"

Tom flew the plane, aiming for the wastebasket across the room. The plane sailed a few feet, then dropped far short of its target.

Kris giggled and stood. "You're such a nut, Tommy. Well, I'd better scoot. I'll meet you downstairs at twelve-thirty." She gave Tom a peck on the cheek and left.

A big, silly smile broke across Lois's face. She knew Kris was making Tom nervous, and she couldn't pass up the chance to tease him a little. "Congratulations, *Tommy,*" she mocked. "I see she's moving into your *cyber*space. That's a big step for you."

Tom shook his head. "Actually, I was planning to take her out to a nice lunch and break up with her today. We've had three dates." He pointed to his rearranged schedule. "*This* is exactly the kind of thing that proves my point. Look at this, Lois." Tom hit a few buttons on his computer and a complex graph appeared. Down one side were names of girls. Across the bottom were numbers. With the computer mouse, Tom demonstrated what the graph meant. "Here's happiness, over time."

"You keep track of this?" Lois asked, amazed.

He continued. "You see how after the third date happiness drops precipitously? Do you know why?"

"I've got an idea," Lois said.

"But you'd be wrong," Tom explained. "It's because at first, everybody's well-behaved and nobody really expects anything too serious to happen. But by date four, it's a relationship—a minefield of secret meanings and unmet expectations. Look at Kris," he said, typing new data into the computer. "Last night was our third date, and she's already downloading schedules!

They start thinking, 'When's he going to marry me? What will our kids look like?' I start thinking, 'Do I have to spend every weekend with her? If I work late is she going to be suspicious?' It's all fighting and making up. Total chaos. When, before that point, it's really rather nice."

Lois knew Tom was a little unevolved, but this was extreme. He obviously had never fallen in love before—when he did, this rule business would be out the window. Until then, Lois couldn't resist playing along. She nodded. "Well, it's hard to argue with the facts."

Tom returned her nod. "I knew you'd appreciate the math of it." That's why he liked Lois; she thought like a man.

"I do, and I believe you've overlooked something."

"I have?"

This time Lois did some fancy math on the computer. "Yes. The only constant in the equation is . . . *you*! The information we need to graph, Tom, is what you do after date three to make everyone . . . miserable."

By the look in Tom's eyes, Lois knew she'd

struck a nerve. Tom wasn't really as cold as he pretended to be. In fact, he was the opposite. He was very sweet, but he was also afraid of being hurt, so he tried hard not to show his true feelings. Whenever he started liking a girl, he'd run the other way; Lois had seen it happen time and time again. She hoped one day some girl wouldn't let him run away so easily.

He looked away from Lois and grabbed a file folder before heading toward the door. "I have a marketing meeting," he said. "See you later."

Lois watched him go. She'd have to be a special girl, Lois thought, to hold on to someone like Tom.

Four

Her mother's handwritten book of recipes sat open on the counter. Amanda had followed the recipe for the secret cream sauce exactly, double-checking each ingredient, measuring and remeasuring, but still the sauce smelled *strange*. She couldn't figure out what she'd done wrong.

"What stinks?" Nolan said as he walked in. Nolan Traynor had been Amanda's best friend for years—even before he'd started helping her in the kitchen.

"Nothing," she said, starting to pour the sauce into the sink.

"No, wait, let me try it," he said, taking the pot from her hands.

"It stinks, you said so yourself."

"Come on." He took the spoon and tasted the sauce thoughtfully. "Yes, it does stink," he said, "but it doesn't taste too bad. Really—"

She took the pot back from him and poured the rest out. "It tastes like bleu cheese and . . . dirt," she muttered.

Nolan gave her a knowing smile. "And there's only one thing worse than that."

"*Rum raisin*," they said together, laughing.

Amanda washed out the saucepan as Nolan tied on his apron. He felt bad for his friend. Stella had just told him the place was closing. He'd been worried that things were going that way. Since he'd come to work a few months earlier, they'd had fewer and fewer customers every day. "Hey, I'm really sorry we have to close, Amanda."

"Stella told you?"

He nodded.

Amanda felt the tears well up again, but she quickly blinked them away.

"Maybe we could get jobs in another restaurant," Nolan said.

"Sure," Amanda said sarcastically, "we'll buy an ad. 'Situations wanted: lousy chef and sous-chef seek restaurant to ruin.'" She left the kitchen with two plates on her arm.

An elderly couple, Ruth and Howard, were sitting at their table—the same table where they had eaten lunch and sometimes dinner for the past thirty years. Like the people in the market, Ruth and Howard had watched Amanda grow up and were like family to her.

"Are you going to want dessert today, Howard?" she asked, serving them their lunch of fettuccine with chicken.

Howard shook his head. "Got my cholesterol results."

Ruth chimed in. "You don't want to know. All I can say is, no more desserts, Howard." Just then the door opened and Bill, the Southern Cross's other regular, came in, carrying a paper bag and a newspaper.

"Hi, everybody. I've got big news! The bodega on the corner's been evicted! Landlord raised the rent on him." Bill sat where he always sat, at the table by the bar. He pulled a sandwich out of the paper bag and opened his newspaper.

"I never liked that guy anyway," Ruth said. Bill stuck out his lower lip. "This neighborhood sure is changing. At least we still have a place to eat, huh?" He took a bite of his sandwich.

Amanda looked at Stella, and Stella looked at Amanda. Stella nodded; Amanda had to break the news to them.

"Well, actually, we have something to tell you," Amanda said. "We're going to have to close the place in a couple of weeks. Our rent was raised too, and we can't make it."

The room was silent. They couldn't believe it. Neither Ruth nor Howard knew how to cook, and for the past thirty years they had been fed by the Southern Cross. Now what would they do? "That's terrible," Ruth said.

"Oh, no . . . where am I going to eat my lunch?" asked Bill.

Amanda sighed. "You bring your own food anyway, Bill. You just eat it in here."

Bill argued, "The coffee's great . . . and Stella's martinis—"

"I love that cheesy chicken!" Howard added.

"Howard, be honest," Amanda said. "You're not here for the food either. You just come here because you're a good, loyal customer. You were when my mother was the cook and the food was good. And you are even though I'm the cook now. And I appreciate that, I really do."

Ruth said, "Don't give up. It's too soon. You'll get better."

"We love you, Amanda," Bill said.

"I love you guys too," Amanda said. "You're all very loyal, very wonderful people, and you deserve a Southern Cross that's like it used to be when Mom was cooking." Her voice cracked. "I tried, but I'm not my mother." She felt terrible, as if she'd let everyone down. She had to get out of that room—she had to get some air.

Tom and Kris had been trying to get a cab for the past ten minutes. It was lunchtime in midtown, when thousands of office workers escaped onto the streets in search of lunch—and often cabs. Tom should have known better than to make a reservation for downtown, but he wanted the lunch to be special, since he was going to break up with Kris.

Tom felt bad, but he figured it was better to do it over a nice lunch, and to do it right away, rather than lead her on and make her think they were a serious item. They had gone out only a few times, but he knew he couldn't fall in love with her. Sometimes he worried that he didn't know how to fall in love, and that love might come along and he'd blow it. But this was not that time.

Kris was gazing at herself in a store window while Tom looked for an available cab on the jammed street. Just when he was about to give up, a cab flicked its OFF DUTY sign off and nearly jumped the curb to pick them up.

The driver was a little old man who could barely see over the dashboard. "Chanterelle," Tom said as they hopped in. "At Hudson and Worth."

"My pleasure," the man said. "If you need anything, my name's Gene. Gene O'Reilly." He smiled and sped off down Fifty-second Street.

Kris opened her cell phone and started to make a call. She smiled apologetically at Tom.

"My personal trainer," she said. "I've got to see if I can see him at five instead of six today. This will only take a sec."

Before they knew it, they were downtown, where the streets were all a jumble. There was a traffic jam. The cab stopped, and Tom got out and paid the driver. As he did, he realized he wasn't where he wanted to be.

"Hey, this isn't Chanterelle," he said.

"Do I have to do *everything* for you?" Gene said. He sped away.

"Where's the restaurant?" Kris asked.

"Don't worry, we'll find it," Tom said.

"Let's ask someone," she suggested.

"No, no, we don't need to—"

Kris crossed the street toward a young woman who was sitting on the curb in front of a small restaurant. "Excuse me, but do you know where Chanterelle is?"

The young woman stood and dusted herself off. Tom caught up with Kris and immediately recognized the young woman—she was the one from the market, the one with the crab.

When Amanda noticed him, she quickly brushed away her tears.

"Hello," Tom said, smiling at her.

His smile was amazing; it made her heart race. "Hello," she managed to say.

"You two know each other?" Kris asked suspiciously.

"Her crab bit me this morning," Tom said.

Kris looked confused. "Really? How nice. Can you tell us where Chanterelle is?"

Amanda thought. "Sure, it's—"

Tom spoke up. "We're here, we might as well just eat. I feel like a little . . . crab. A little of *that* crab. It's only fair, don't you think?"

"Uh, lunch is sort of over," Amanda said, and thought *forever, at my restaurant.*

"So you were just teasing me?" Tom asked.

"What?" Amanda said.

"What?" Kris said.

He explained, "I mean in the market, with the stuff about the crab napoleon and the souf-flé. . . ."

Amanda smiled weakly and opened the door.

What's one more humiliation? she asked herself, and she waved them inside.

Ruth and Howard looked at Kris and Tom as if they were aliens. Bill set down his newspaper and stared, until Amanda gestured for him to act cool. Once the couple was seated, she hustled into the kitchen, her heart racing.

"He's here!" she cried to Nolan. "Oh my god, I can't believe it! He's waiting for me to cook crab napoleon and I don't even know what it is!"

Nolan looked at her as if she was speaking a foreign language. "Say what?"

"This guy from the market. He's so cute, Nolan, and I told him I could make some fabulous thing and now he showed up!"

"So tell him we're out of crab whatever. Tell him we're closed."

"I can't do that."

"Want me to?"

"No. Then he'll leave."

"That's the idea, isn't it?"

Amanda shook a spatula at Nolan. "No! I want him to stay."

Nolan rolled his eyes. "Okay. Then we'll make it. Crab . . . Crab what?" He looked around the kitchen for the ingredients, unsure of what they needed.

"Napoleon!" Amanda was in such a panic that she got the giggles.

"You go upstairs and dig up a recipe," Nolan said. "I'll start cleaning these things up."

Amanda flew out the back door. Nolan fired up a stove burner under a big pot of water and looked at the basket of crabs. "*Right*. Crab napoleon? This is gonna suck," he said. And as he reached for the basket, one feisty little crab jumped out and scurried under the refrigerator.

Meanwhile, Amanda was standing on a footstool, trying to reach a box of recipes stored high on a shelf in the closet of her apartment above the restaurant. Finally her fingertips grabbed the little wooden box, and she immediately flipped open its lid and started riffling through the cards.

There, caught between two recipe cards, she found her mother's diamond earrings!

Amanda stared at them, amazed. She hadn't seen these in years . . . and hadn't that man in the market just mentioned them? What a strange coincidence.

She got down from the footstool and looked at the picture of her mother that rested on the mantel; in it her mother was wearing the earrings. Amanda put them on and looked at her reflection in a mirror. "I wish I had another chance," she said. "Just one more." A breeze ruffled Amanda's hair, and she walked out, forgetting the box of recipes.

Down in the restaurant, Kris and Tom were squirming under the curious stares of the regulars.

"I've never been to a place like this," Kris said. "There's nobody here. The food must be terrible."

"It's late for lunch," Tom said, defending the place.

"The decor is so . . . *Cleveland*," she said in a snooty voice.

Just then Amanda popped her head in from the kitchen. "Sorry for the delay—it'll be just a few more minutes. Are you having crab too?" she asked Kris.

"Nooo, I don't think so," Kris said with a sneer. "Could you do something very simple, like grilled chicken, with absolutely nothing on it? I eat seafood only in three-star restaurants," she said, adding a fake smile.

"No problem," Amanda replied. She charged back into the kitchen. "One chicken paillard for the mistake he's with," she said to Nolan. "Girls like that really bug me."

Nolan went to check out this guy who had Amanda all worked up. "That's the guy?" he asked. "Big deal. He's smooth outside, but nothing's under the hood. Look at the girl he's with. She's perfect for him."

"No, she's not."

"Check out the hair. Every strand in place, just like his," Nolan said.

"I can fix my hair," Amanda said, her hand tucking in a wild tendril.

"Not like that, you can't," Nolan said helpfully.

Amanda slapped a chicken breast on the counter. "So she has perfect hair! Big deal!"

Nolan continued, "It's not just the hair, it's her skin too. She's got that kind of skin . . ."

Amanda pounded the chicken with a mallet. "It's makeup. Are you going to help me here or what?"

Nolan came back to the counter and started prepping the salads. "You gotta be born with that kind of skin. And that black suit's so sharp you could cut yourself on it. She's got the shoes, the handbag . . . she's all put together."

Amanda was getting really mad now. "Nolan, shut up, okay? You're wrong. He's not happy with her. He doesn't belong with somebody with"—she pounded the chicken—"perfect hair! And perfect skin!" She pounded the chicken again. "And a perfect wardrobe! With matching shoes!" She slammed the chicken on the grill. "And if you can't see that, well, I feel sorry for you."

Nolan stared at his friend, amazed at her outburst. The little crab that had escaped under the refrigerator came out to see what all the fuss was about.

Amanda herself was a little surprised by her

tirade. "I'm just under a lot of stress today," she said. She straightened her apron, wiped her brow, and took a deep breath. "But I can take it. Now I'm going to make the most delicious crab napoleon." The little crab scurried away and hid again.

"Where's the recipe?" Nolan asked.

Amanda tossed up her hands. "I couldn't find one. But desperate times require desperate measures, right?"

Nolan looked at his friend. She sure was acting strange. He shrugged and continued to work.

"For once in my life I'd like to make something really great," Amanda said as she prepared the dish. "Just have everything come together so perfectly that just one bite is ecstasy. Have you ever noticed how many words there are for 'delicious'?" As she cooked, she recited all the words she knew. "Savory, tasty, scrumptious," she said as she sliced, spiced, and chopped the ingredients. "Delectable, succulent, mouthwatering," she added as she whisked and grated.

When she was done, she looked at her

creation in awe: it was a beautiful rectangle of layered crab, tomato, and creamy sauce. It looked, quite simply, *delicious*. "Nolan . . . ," she said, stunned.

Nolan thought she was asking for the obligatory garnish of parsley. When he turned and saw what she had made, he too was stunned. "Wow," he mumbled.

Just then Stella blew into the kitchen. "The people-we-don't-know want their food," she said breathlessly, reaching for the plate with the crab napoleon. She stopped in her tracks when she saw it. "Where the heck did this come from?"

"I don't know," Amanda said, mystified. She'd never made anything so beautiful.

Stella picked up the plate. "Well, I hope you can do it again, because *I* want one. It looks amazing!" She left with the two lunches. Before the kitchen door had swung shut, the little crab made its getaway into the dining room.

Tom took a bite of his crab napoleon. It was incredibly tasty. He took another bite, just to be sure. It was absolutely delicious. He suddenly felt overjoyed, happy, ecstatic even. "Oh, my, this is so . . ." He had to have another bite. He was transported. "Savory. Tasty."

Stella served Howard coffee, and together they anxiously watched Tom and Kris eating. "New customers, Stella," he said. "Maybe it's a sign."

Suddenly Kris started coughing and choking.

"Yeah," Stella sighed. "A sign that we should have closed yesterday."

"Are you okay?" Tom asked Kris.

"I think so." She took another bite. "You're such a controlling jerk," she said.

"What?"

"I'm sorry!" Kris put her hand over her mouth. "I don't know why I said that."

"Me either," he replied. He prepared a forkful of crab napoleon for her—"You've really got to try this. It's . . . It's scrumptious!"—and then put it in his own mouth, so eager was he to taste the dish again. "No, it's delectable!"

Amanda stood behind a pillar near the kitchen, watching these new customers eat her food. She noticed that Tom used her own words—*savory* and *delectable*—and she thought it was another strange coincidence.

Kris continued to eat the chicken, chewing hard, her face darkening. "You know, *Tommy*, I feel like I'm suddenly seeing you for the first time."

"Really?" Tom asked, not sure what she meant.

"Yes," Kris went on, "which is why I'm asking myself: What *am* I doing with someone like you? *Me*, with my *perfect* hair?" Kris then stood up as if possessed and threw her plate of food against the wall. "I hate this place!" she bellowed.

Tom was stunned. He'd never seen Kris like this. Sure, she was a little obnoxious sometimes, but she'd never been downright rude or violent. "Kris! What are you doing?" He turned to the other customers. "Please excuse us. "

"I'll do whatever I want!" Kris said.

"Within reason!" Tom said.

"I'll give you a reason! A really good one!" she hollered. "I have perfect skin!"

When Amanda heard *that* she knew it wasn't

a coincidence. Something very weird was going on, and she had no idea what it was or why it was happening.

"None of these dishes match!" Kris said, throwing another plate. Howard and Ruth ducked. So did the little crab, which had managed to get out of the kitchen only to be caught in this food-fight cross fire. It hid under a table. Stella rushed over to try to calm the deranged woman.

"A glass of wine on the house? To soothe your nerves." Stella offered Kris a glass, placing it on the table. Kris backhanded it into the wall.

"A simple 'No, thank you' would do," Stella muttered, walking away.

Kris continued her rage against Tom. "You're a perfect waste of my perfect wardrobe! With matching shoes!"

Tom stared at her, aghast. "Kris, nobody's *that* perfect."

"I am!" she declared. "And if you can't see that, well, then I feel sorry for you." On her way out of the restaurant, Kris heaved the remaining plates off the other tables. Ruth, Howard, and Bill all cowered as she passed.

Amanda came out from behind the pillar. "Is everybody okay?" she asked. Stella and Nolan started cleaning up. Amanda looked at Tom, who had a dreamy expression on his face, despite what had just happened. "She has quite a temper," Amanda said.

"Not usually. It's my Curse of the Fourth Date." Tom noticed how pretty Amanda was. He liked her long, wild hair and sparkly brown eyes. He liked her sweet, open face. He liked just looking at her.

"What?" Amanda asked.

"Just a theory of mine. I'm very sorry about . . . *this*. I'll be glad to replace everything." He took one last bite of his lunch. He felt light-headed, as if he was floating. He couldn't take his eyes off Amanda. "What was in this? My name's Tom, by the way. *Dill*."

"Tom Dill?" Amanda asked.

"Tom Bartlett. Did you use dill?" he asked.

"Like the pear," Amanda said with a smile.

"Send me the *bill*," Tom said. "That rhymes with *dill*, doesn't it?"

"Yes. And I *will*." She smiled. He smiled back, and she too felt light-headed.

"Good one," he said, not wanting to stop. What else rhymed with *dill*? And then he caught himself. *What am I doing?* Tom suddenly felt completely confused, and that was not like him. He prided himself on always staying in control. What was going on? He wanted to get out of there, but he also wanted to keep talking to this beautiful girl. He felt completely addled. He stood. "Really, I'm very sorry about all this. Here's my card. I want to replace everything. I'd really better go." He stole one last glance at Amanda as he hurried out the door.

Stella looked at the mess and declared, "So much for walk-ins." She carried a handful of broken plates back into the kitchen.

Amanda knelt and picked up some more, going over the day's events in her mind. Something weird *was* going on. No doubt about it. From the coin seemingly suspended in midair to the peculiar old crab man at the market to her suddenly incredible cooking to the young woman's crazy behavior in the restaurant, the day had been full of strange surprises that Amanda knew could not be mere coincidences.

But what were they? And why were they happening today, to her?

"Maybe I will have some dessert, after all," Howard sighed. "Just to settle my nerves."

Amanda smiled and went into the kitchen to make her oldest customer something very special.

Five

"*What happened to you at lunch?*" Lois asked, shocked at the sight of her boss as he walked through Bendel's grand Fifth Avenue entrance. Tom was the best-dressed man she had ever seen, always as immaculate and perfectly groomed as a GQ model. But right then he looked as if he'd been caught in a Cuisinart. There was food all over his beautiful suit and even flecks of *something* in his hair.

He said dreamily, "I had the most incredible lunch."

"Too bad you didn't get any of it in your mouth," she said.

"No, this is Kris's lunch," he said, still in a fog. He moved up the sweeping staircase as if he was sleepwalking.

"So I guess she didn't take it too well," Lois commented, walking beside him.

"What?"

"Your breaking up with her."

"She totally freaked out," Tom said. "And then *she* dumped *me*. If the food hadn't made me feel so good, I'd be really upset right now."

"But you wanted to break up with her," Lois said, confused.

"I do have feelings, Lois," he explained. "I mean, she acted like I was nothing. I wonder if she ever liked me. She might have just been using me."

Tom headed toward his boss's office, with its big doors marked JONATHAN BENDEL.

Lois took his arm, holding him back. "What are you doing? You can't go in there like that." She pulled him away from the double doors and marched him to his office and directly into his closet, where a row of ten identical blue suits hung. "Let's see," she said dryly. "A *blue* suit? Or a blue *suit*? Or—I know—*the* blue suit."

Lois handed Tom one of the suits and turned her back while he changed. She primped in the full-length mirror, touching her hair.

Tom observed her. "It's been two years, Lois. Jonathan's not biting. You should move on."

"I can't. I'm crazy about him," Lois sighed. She was. She had been hopelessly in love with Jonathan since before she worked at Bendel's. And he acted as if she didn't exist.

"What do you see that I don't?" he asked.

She couldn't explain it. Jonathan was awkward and shy and possibly even a little bit stupid, but Lois felt a powerful desire for him, and it had not abated in years. She didn't understand it herself, but then, she didn't need to; she simply felt what she felt and accepted it. She smiled just thinking about Jonathan.

Tom was waiting for a reply. When he saw that dopey smile spread across Lois's face, he took that as the answer. "Okay, okay, forget I asked."

She looked at him. "You're my friend. Help me. If I could figure out what Jonathan's weakness is, I might be able to seduce him."

"That's easy," Tom said. "Immortality."

"Immortality?"

"He wants it more than anything. And *his*, not his grandfather Henri's, who opened this store. Jonathan's desperate for it."

"Great. How can I use that?" she asked.

They strolled into Jonathan's office. The conference table was surrounded by executives, but the room was dead quiet. Jonathan did not look happy. "Nice of you to join us," he grumbled as Tom and Lois entered.

"Sorry I'm late. Please, go on," Tom said.

"Fine," Jonathan answered in a clipped tone. "Tom? Why did you spend a hundred thousand dollars on a floor that makes me dizzy? All those black and white stripes across the dance floor create an optical illusion that makes the floor seem a bit wavy, don't you think? And all around it are those dinner tables on three levels of risers. Which also make me dizzy. And let's not forget about those mirrors. . . . The place doesn't look like a restaurant—it looks like a set for an MGM musical!"

Tom didn't back down. "That's exactly right, Jonathan. It is a stage—a stage for every diner's fantasy. To create a unique, romantic, and utterly unforgettable dining experience. And that floor, like a *crab*, can help create that mood."

Everyone looked at Tom strangely. Like a

crab? Why was he talking about a crab? Lois kicked him under the table.

Tom ignored her and continued, "We want Jonathan's to be the coolest restaurant these jaded New Yorkers have ever seen, and to do that we have to be lavish. Sometimes you have to go the extra mile to get the extra diller—I mean *dollar*." Tom shook his head. All he could think about was that crab concoction . . . and the girl who'd made it.

"I don't like the sound of this," Jonathan said sharply.

"Have I ever let you down?" Tom asked.

"Not yet. But you're young. Very young," his boss answered.

Lois leaned over and looked into Jonathan's eyes. "Imagine your *fame*, Jonathan, when this is the most talked-about place in town. There'll be articles about you in *People* and *Vanity Fair*. You'll be *immortal*."

Jonathan listened, entranced. "I like you, Lois. You're like a man. You think with your guts."

Lois sagged. It wasn't exactly the kind of compliment she'd been hoping for.

Tom thought about Amanda and felt as if he was missing her already, but that was *ridiculous*—he didn't even know the girl. Her eyes and smile were so warm and sweet . . . *"Owww!"* Tom cried. Lois had just kicked him under the table again.

"Tom," Lois said through a tight smile.

Then he remembered where he was—in the staff meeting—and focused his thoughts on work.

Lois prompted him. "Jonathan was just asking you about the fall catalog."

"Oh, right," Tom said. "The fall catalog . . ."

Six

Stella blotted her lipstick and grabbed her purse. She was going to the Blue Bonnet, a fun late-night restaurant that was always crowded with other waiters and cooks, as well as theater people who got off work around midnight and were not yet ready for bed. Stella hoped to convince Amanda to come with her, but she wasn't optimistic. Her niece was so smart and sweet and beautiful, it drove Stella nuts that she hadn't fallen in love yet. Or even in like. And how would she, if she never left that kitchen?

Stella walked down the back stairs, through the kitchen, and into the dining room. Amanda sat in a booth reading cookbooks. "Time for fun," Stella said. "Antonio's bringing his cousin, and Amanda, he's very cute. . . ."

Amanda scanned a recipe. "You go on. Tell Antonio I said hi."

"Why are you reading those?"

"I feel like trying something new," Amanda said. "Today that crab napoleon turned out so great, maybe I should experiment more often, and then we wouldn't have to—" Amanda stopped. She didn't want to get her hopes up too high. But after lunch today, she felt as if she could pull off anything if she really tried.

"You're right. You should keep trying," Stella said, as if she could read Amanda's mind. "And it's good to get your hopes up. That's what hope is for, to motivate us to do things we're not sure we can."

"I want to make an incredible dessert," Amanda declared. "What's the best dessert you ever ate?"

Stella smiled, remembering. "A caramel éclair in Paris, with Michel. It was August first, 1968, and we were sitting in a little café. It was the most wonderful thing I ever tasted. Very hard to make, though." She walked to the front door. "Don't stay up too late, sweetie. Chefs need sleep too." She left the restaurant.

Amanda kept reading the cookbook. She was studying a recipe when the door blew open and a breeze fluttered the pages of the book. Then, just as suddenly, the door slammed shut.

Amanda stood. "Well, if that's not a sign I don't know what is," she said. She closed the door and headed into the kitchen with new resolve. She was going to make caramel éclairs— *without* a recipe. She'd cooked without a recipe at lunch, why not now?

Puff! The flour billowed out of the bag as Amanda slammed it on the counter. The crab scuttled out from behind a mixing bowl. "Hey, where'd you come from?" Amanda said. "You're the same little guy from the market, aren't you?" The crab's eyes seemed to bob up and down on their stalks. "You probably could use some water, couldn't you?" Amanda filled a saucer, and the crab crawled in.

For the next few hours Amanda was engrossed in preparing the éclairs. She whisked egg yolks and sugar and then watched the mixture boil into a golden custard that seemed to shine and make her diamond earrings sparkle. In another pot she made the caramel, then dropped a trickle of the dark syrup into the cooling custard, drawing bigger and bigger circles. And all the time she thought about Tom. He was a stranger to her, but she felt she already knew him, as if they had been friends before. She saw past his fine clothes and cool demeanor and knew that inside he was as sweet and wonderful as the custard she was making. She didn't know how or why she knew this, but she did. And while she cut the pastry into strips and baked it, and while she piped the caramelized custard into the éclairs, she dreamt of being with him and hoped her cooking would make him understand and feel the way she did.

She held a finished éclair in her hand and took a bite.

Delicious.

Nearly swooning, she took another bite, and even as she found herself leaning against the wall and sliding to the floor, she felt as if she was floating.

The next morning Nolan was surprised to see the mess in the kitchen—and no Amanda. It wasn't like her to leave the place such a wreck, or not to be there. He ran up the back stairs, calling out her name. Finally he tapped on the door of her bedroom, then peeked in. She was brushing her hair, an otherworldly look on her face.

"Looks like love to me," he laughed. "And like somebody came back for some dessert!"

"I wish!" she said, opening her closet door. She held out a blue blouse. "How's this?" she asked.

"For what?"

"For buying plates. Uptown." Amanda added a floral vest.

"Forget the vest," Nolan said. "Plates? What do we need plates for? We're closing, aren't we?"

"Well, Tom offered to buy us plates. It'd be rude not to accept," Amanda said coolly.

"Tom?"

"That's his name."

"The one with the psycho girlfriend? Yeah, I guess that *would* be rude," Nolan said, teasing.

"We're not closing for a couple of weeks. We need plates, don't we?" she asked.

Nolan cocked his head. "Sure, sure. But we do have about three left. One for Howard, one for Ruth, and one for Bill, so we could manage—"

"Nolan!" She knew he was just trying to bug her. She held out a black sweater.

"That's fine," he said.

"So when I get there, what do I talk about? You saw him, and you know me, and you know how I can run on when I get nervous, and I will be nervous, uptown, with someone like him, you know . . ." She held out a long flowered skirt for Nolan's opinion.

"I like that. It doesn't matter, just be your-self."

Amanda stepped into the closet and began changing her outfit. "That's exactly what I'm afraid of," she explained. "Come on, you're a guy, what are guys interested in?"

Nolan rubbed his chin. "There are five things. Sex, cars, sports, money, and sex."

"Come on."

"I saw it on *Dateline*," Nolan informed her. "The average man thinks about sex two hundred and thirty-eight times a day."

Amanda came out of the closet, wearing *all* the clothes Nolan had approved. All the colors and patterns and scarves she had put on seemed at once odd and wonderful together. She gave Nolan a quizzical look. "But that means they think about sex all day."

"Sure."

"Maybe that applies to *you*," she said.

"You know how men are always adjusting their pants, or holding their belts and stuff?" Nolan asked.

"Yeah . . ."

"Well, that's when they're thinking about it," Nolan informed her.

Amanda clapped a hand to her cheek. "Oh, no, why did you tell me that? Now it's in my head forever. Every time I see a guy doing that I'll wonder . . ."

Nolan started down the stairs. Amanda stopped him to ask what he thought of her outfit. "So?"

He smiled broadly and played with his belt.

Amanda let out a loud laugh. "Good!"

Bendel's was the most elegant department store in New York City. Standing proudly on Fifth Avenue, just south of Fifty-seventh Street, with a four-story etched-glass window, the hundred-year-old store offered only the finest clothes and home furnishings from around the world. Amanda paused in front of the huge glass-and-brass doors. The doorman did not acknowledge her, which made her feel even more insecure.

"Excuse me," she began, and the doorman opened the door.

Amanda stood in the central atrium and looked up at the crystal chandelier and the black railings that lined the balconies on each floor. Bendel's was more like a palace than a department store. Everywhere she looked the most beautiful objects—makeup, scarves, jewelry, and clothing—were displayed for sale. Amanda was overwhelmed as she wandered farther into the store.

"There, that's perfect now," Tom said as he placed the last scarf on a tall, elaborate display. Hundreds of scarves were draped in an intricate pattern over a wire tree. Ramos, an assistant manager, thanked Tom for his help and went back to his counter. Tom proceeded up the central staircase until he heard a loud *crash!* He looked down to see the tree in shambles on the floor, and a girl covered in scarves. He rushed to help her.

Amanda looked up from under the scarves and to her horror saw it was Tom.

"I guess this makes us even," he said. "I mean, for the plates."

Amanda's face reddened. "Oh, yes . . . I guess so. I'm so sorry. I turned around and . . ." She felt like a clumsy fool.

"It's okay," Tom said. He thanked Ramos for helping clean up and led Amanda away. "This is a nice coincidence," he said. "Do you shop here a lot?"

Amanda gasped. "Oh, no. I've never been here before. It's incredible. All of this is so, so . . . elegant." She was still in awe. She noticed that Tom was looking at her askance. "You did say you'd replace the plates?" she asked. "That's why I'm here."

Tom ran a hand down his lapel. "Yes . . . of course. I just thought you'd send me the bill . . . but this is fine. I'm glad you came up."

"You are?"

He looked at her and smiled. "Yes," he said, taking her elbow. "Come, I'll show you our great china department."

The mere touch of his hand sent goose bumps down her neck. As they walked up the sweeping staircase, Amanda noted that several people said hello to Tom or asked him to sign documents; he was clearly an important person at Bendel's.

They browsed through the shelves of plates. There were so many beautiful choices, Amanda worried she wouldn't be able to make a decision.

"I am sorry about yesterday," Tom said.

"Is your girlfriend okay?" Amanda asked.

"Yes. That was so weird. She never acted like that before."

"Did you do something to provoke her?"

"No," Tom said. "Did you?"

Amanda gulped. She had been thinking about *that* very possibility ever since she'd heard her own thoughts coming out of the girl's mouth. But that was crazy. It *must* have been a coincidence.

"But I guess you should know she's not my girlfriend anymore," Tom said, immediately wondering why he was telling her that.

"Oh, no . . . I'm sorry," Amanda said. But she had to admit she was a little glad.

"It's okay. We didn't get along, really."

Amanda had chosen six different patterns. "I'll take eight of each of these, please."

Tom looked at the plates, confused. "But they don't match."

"So?"

"I see. . . . That's bold." He told the saleswoman to send him the bill, and they drifted out of the china department. "It explains your outfit," he said teasingly.

"To eliminate this scarf would have taken another half hour," Amanda said, laughing. "Doesn't look like it takes you very long," she teased him back.

"I seem to come out of the shower fully dressed in a blue suit."

"And a belt?"

He looked at her, confused again. "Well, no, actually. I don't wear a belt."

Amanda was surprised. "Really?"

He gave her an odd look. "No. Why? Does it matter?"

Amanda bit her lip. "Never mind." She should have known this would happen! Nolan had put that idea in her head, and because of it she'd just blurted out something stupid. "So," she said, quickly changing the subject, "you said you're opening a restaurant too? But you work here, right?"

"We're opening one in the store," Tom said. "But come on, you can't ask me something so bizarre like whether I wear a belt and not tell me why you want to know."

Amanda tilted her head. "I don't really care whether you—"

"Then why ask? And why not tell me why you did?"

"Okay, okay," she said, giving up. "My friend Nolan told me this thing about men and sex. They think about it two hundred and thirty-eight times a day, and when they do they play with their belts."

"That's ridiculous!" Tom exclaimed.

She was relieved to hear that he felt that way. "That's what I thought."

He looked at Amanda. "I mean, just do the numbers." He started calculating in his head, and as he did he folded an order form into an elaborate paper airplane. "I'm awake for about seventeen hours a day," he said. "Divided by two hundred and thirty-eight, that means I'd be having a sexual thought about every four minutes." He stood for a second, and then the thought hit him: "Well, yes. I guess that is about right. More or less."

Amanda looked at her watch. "I can't believe that!"

"Why not?"

"A good sexual thought takes at least twenty minutes," she announced.

"Really?" he said weakly.

Suddenly she noticed his airplane. "That's an interesting sweepback," she said.

"How do you know about paper airplanes?"

"I hated algebra. Does it fly?"

Tom held it up. "Sure, it can fly, but never where I want. Look, I'm going for that basket," he said, and shot the airplane toward a basket full of soap. The airplane did not make the basket, but it did do an incredible loop-the-loop before shooting straight into a woman's beehive hairdo. "It may not fly far, but it flies with purpose," Tom said. He laughed, and his face relaxed and lit up.

Just then a salesperson tapped him on the shoulder, breaking into their moment together. "Mr. Bartlett, your secretary is looking for you. The Wilkinson meeting is starting."

Tom looked at his watch. "Thank you, Helen."

Amanda backed off a step. "I'm sorry. I've made you late—"

Tom held up a hand. "No, it's fine really. I'll walk you to the elevators." On their way they passed through Evening Wear. Tom noticed Amanda eyeing a beautiful pink satin gown that was displayed on a mannequin. It was his favorite in the store.

"It's beautiful, isn't it?" he said.

"Oh, yes," she breathed. She'd never worn anything so fine. She'd never been anywhere where she could!

"You'd look great in that," he said.

Amanda blushed. "Thanks . . . it is awfully nice."

They waited for the elevator. Amanda wished she didn't have to leave so soon, just when he was warming up to her.

"I'm really glad you came up," he said.

"You are? Me too," she responded.

"You smell good," he said, and she remembered she had brought something for him. She reached into her big bag and brought out a pink bakery box from the restaurant.

"Your lunch came with dessert," she said.

He opened the box and saw four caramel éclairs. They looked delicious, but he handed the box back to her. "Thank you, but I don't eat dessert."

She stared at him, surprised. "Really? I love dessert. It's the whole point of the meal. Sometimes I have to have dessert first because I can't wait—"

Ping!

The elevator doors opened and they stepped inside. Amanda hit the button for the first floor.

She held up the box, flipping back the lid. "You sure you don't want a bite?"

He smiled. "Oh, okay," he conceded, "I'll just try one." He carefully lifted one of the pastries from the box and sank his teeth into it. He began chewing, instantly feeling a wave of happiness washing through him.

"You like it?" Amanda asked.

He did. *A lot.* He nodded, still chewing. "It's . . . very . . . gooooood," he said, taking another bite. The elevator stopped at a floor, and Brian, the shoe department manager, stepped on.

"Hello, Mr. Bartlett," Brian said. Tom nodded to him, ecstasy spreading through him as he finished the first éclair. He lifted a second from the box and took a bite, smiling at Amanda as he did. "These are great," he said softly. "Have you met Brian? Brian's in shoes." Tom couldn't believe how exquisite these pastries were.

"Nice to meet you. I'm Amanda," she said.

Dreamily Tom took another bite of the éclair. He looked at Brian. "Oh, boy, do I love shoes." Tom looked as if he was about to swoon.

Brian looked at him, pleased at the attention from the boss. "Me too, Mr. Bartlett."

Tom licked the caramel off his fingers and smiled giddily. "I love that we *sell* them. I love that we sell them in *twos*. It's so . . . *Noah's Ark*!" Tom giggled like a little kid.

Amanda giggled too, wondering what had gotten into Tom; he was sounding crazy.

The elevator opened on the first floor. Tom shoved Brian out and said, "Change of plan." He hit the button for Jonathan's and the doors closed, leaving them alone in the small elevator together.

"Where are we going?" Amanda asked. "Are you all right?"

Tom couldn't believe how wonderful he felt. "Yeah! I feel great! You've got to have one of these." He fed her an éclair, and suddenly she felt ecstatic too.

They arrived at the entrance of the restaurant, which was still under construction. He led her to the kitchen, and they peeked through the double doors. Valderon, the head chef Amanda had seen at the market, was yelling in French at his battalion of assistants, the sous-chefs. "Imbeciles! My pet poodle cooks better than you!" He spit at them.

Amanda and Tom stifled a laugh and headed into the dining room.

The room was glorious. The black-and-white dance floor surrounded by mirrors, the intimate dining tables, the crystal chandeliers created a most elegant, lavish atmosphere. And the room wasn't even finished.

"It's incredible," Amanda said, gazing around.

"No, *this* is incredible," Tom said, holding up the éclair. "The way it starts in your mouth . . . and then it travels to your brain, and then—then all of a sudden it races down your spine and then it explodes out of your toes!" His eyes shone brightly. He fed Amanda another éclair and stood close to her.

They seemed to start swaying, and then they heard music. Without thinking, Tom took Amanda in his arms and twirled her onto the dance floor. A swing band appeared out of nowhere, and the music swelled. They glided to-gether as if they had been professional partners for years, dancing so beautifully, their feet seemed to barely touch the floor. Amanda did a double take when she saw the band, but she kept dancing, delighted to be in Tom's arms, until—

"*Am I interrupting something?*" Jonathan said gruffly. A group of suited men stood behind him.

The music had stopped. The band had disappeared.

"Bartlett!" Jonathan barked. "The Wilkinson group wants to see the restaurant." He pulled Tom aside. "What are you doing? Interviewing waitresses?" he hissed.

Tom was completely confused. *What was he doing?* Dancing in the middle of the day? He didn't even know how to dance! And where had the band come from—and where had it gone? He looked at Amanda. "I'm sorry, I really have to go now."

–She smiled mischievously. "Okay . . . thanks. It was fun. Wasn't it?" she asked. He nodded and she continued, nervous and excited, "That's good, because that means it probably would be fun again, at least I think so. . . . It's only logical, right? If we got together again—"

"I'll call you," Tom said, smiling.

"You will?" she asked, surprised.

"Of course," he answered, and he walked away with Jonathan and the businessmen.

Amanda watched him go, hoping he was feeling what she was feeling, and that it wouldn't be too long before she saw him again.

Seven

The days went by, and Tom didn't call.
But there was good news: Business at the restaurant had picked up significantly. Word had traveled fast about a new food hot spot, and New Yorkers had started coming to find out for themselves. The customers came, ate wonderful meals, and left delighted. And they, in turn, sent more people to the Southern Cross. Amanda kept experimenting with new recipes, making up new combinations, and the customers loved everything she concocted.

But Amanda didn't feel as thrilled as she should. She was disappointed not to hear from Tom. As she stood over the stove, she wondered why he didn't call. When she woke up in the morning and when she went to sleep at night she wondered what had happened. That day at Bendel's had seemed so magical to her—and she had thought he had felt it too. It didn't seem possible that he didn't feel the way she did. And if that was so, then why wouldn't he want to see her?

"Five days is definitely a brush-off," she said to Nolan as they chopped and sliced vegetables. "Maybe he got back together with the Perfect Girl."

Nolan sliced through a tomato. "Just call him yourself," he said. "It's the late nineties. I think it's okay for the girl to call the guy sometimes—"

Amanda tossed some vegetables into a skillet with oil and watched them sizzle. "No way. That would scare him. It's better to wait."

Nolan slammed his knife down and picked up the cordless phone. "I can't bear another day of this moaning," he grumbled. He handed the phone to her. She took it and hid it in a drawer. Nolan went after it, but Amanda backed in front of the cabinet, blocking him.

Stella walked in through the kitchen door and noted that the two chefs were doing no work. "What's going on? We've got a dining room full of hungry people out there," she yelled. She placed a few more orders on the counter, picked up a couple of finished dinners, then rushed back out to the dining room.

Amanda went back to the vegetables in the sauté pan, flipping them with a shake of the pan's handle.

Nolan took the opportunity to grab the phone from the drawer and dial 411. "The number for Bendel's, please," he said.

Uptown at the store, Tom and Lois were busy going over her department's budget in his office.

Lois peeked over his shoulder. "Tom . . . ?" she said in a singsong voice.

"Yes, Lois . . ." He examined the papers on his desk.

"There's a juicy rumor going around about you. I'm trying to kill it, of course."

"Thank you," he said casually. He hated being the subject of gossip, or even of *conversation*. Because he was the manager of the store, some of it was inevitable, but that didn't make him like it. "Why do you need to hire another buyer?" he asked, changing the subject.

"Don't you want to know what the rumor's about?" Lois prodded. "*Good*, I'll tell you. It's about you and a girl—*in flagrante*—up in the restaurant." Lois could barely contain her excitement.

"'*In flagrante*'? We were dancing," Tom said.

Lois laughed. "*Dancing?* That's even better! That's so sweet."

"It wasn't me," Tom said irritably. He'd been distracted by thoughts of that afternoon with Amanda ever since she'd left. And he was not one to let women interfere with his work, no matter how much or how little he cared for them. He had always been able to keep his emotions under control, but here he was, unable to focus on anything. His work was suffering, and he was baffled.

"Who was it, then?" Lois teased.

Tom laid the budget report aside and gave her a bewildered look. "I mean, I felt like I was somebody else, you know?" he said, trying to explain. "I felt like somebody"—he was at a loss for the word, but then it came to him—"*romantic*. I don't know what happened to make me that kind of a guy, but I definitely wasn't myself." He sat still for a second, remembering how magical the moment had been.

Lois sat on the corner of the desk and gave him a pat on the head. "How nice for you . . . or *not*. I don't know," she said, stifling a smile. Whoever this girl was, she had Tom in a spell such as Lois had never seen before. It was sweet and exciting to watch her cool friend melt before her very eyes. "What's her name?" she asked demurely.

The voice of Tom's secretary interrupted from the telephone intercom: "Amanda Shelton on line one, Mr. Bartlett."

From the look of terror in Tom's eyes, Lois knew that *this* was the girl. "Ooooooh, scary," she said, gathering her papers with a small laugh. "I guess she doesn't need to download anything on her computer, does she?"

Tom shooed Lois out of the room and with some trepidation picked up the phone. He had promised to call and hadn't; Amanda might be a bit sore at him. And what did he want with her, anyway? He thought he didn't want to see her again, he was already so confused by his feelings; yet he also found he was thrilled that she'd called. "Hello?" he said timidly.

"Hello," Amanda said. She leaned on the counter, looking daggers at Nolan for getting her into this predicament. She knew what it meant when the guy didn't call—it meant he wasn't interested. She was just asking for more rejection. "It's Amanda," she said, hoping he already knew that.

"Oh, hi," he said, dreading what might come next. "How've you been?"

"Oh, fine, fine. Busy, actually. Busier than usual."

"That's good, right?"

"Yes, it's great. I can't understand it, but it's nice," she said, feeling like a complete jerk. She wanted to get it over with, so she just charged on. "You should come by sometime, I mean, if you'd like to have dinner at the restaurant, maybe tonight even—"

"Tonight?" He panicked. He didn't want to say no, but he didn't want to say yes. What was wrong with him? He looked at his calendar and saw that he was free. But the fact that he was so confused made him want to avoid the cause of this confusion—which was Amanda. "I'm sorry, I have a business dinner," he lied.

Amanda persevered, feeling pathetic. "Well, I'm here late if you feel like dropping by after or something, or maybe not, maybe some other time."

"Sure."

"Well, I'd better get back to work," she said.

"Yeah, don't let anything burn," Tom said, trying to be funny and feeling like a jerk. He said goodbye and hung up. Why hadn't he just said "Yes, I'd love to come by for some dinner?" What *was* he so afraid of? And why couldn't he get over the fear?

Amanda hung up the phone and glared at Nolan. "Thanks a lot," she said.

Nolan prepared a plate for a diner. "So he's busy this evening. Maybe another night," he said.

Amanda sprinkled spices on a piece of tuna. "Maybe he's not interested—which I already knew," she muttered. She poured some oil in a pan, took the tuna, and seared it on the grill. She tossed some julienned vegetables into the pan along with it.

The day passed as she cooked lunches, and the night passed as she cooked dinners, and suddenly it was closing time and she sat slumped in a booth, counting the day's take. Stella wiped down the bar.

"We did a hundred dinners tonight," Amanda told her, amazed.

Stella smiled, impressed. "I don't know what got into you, but it's good. They say fear is a great motivator. I guess being afraid we were going to lose the place has brought out the best in you."

"I don't think it was fear," Amanda answered.

"What, then?" Stella asked. She got her coat off a rack near the door.

Amanda thought the answer was actually love, that her feelings for Tom, as irrational and unrequited as they seemed to be, had come out in the food she'd made for him, and had continued to get into her cooking ever since. The strange events of that day—meeting the crab man and his crab (which was still scuttling around her kitchen), and finding her mother's diamond earrings—seemed to play a role in Amanda's improved cooking, but what role she didn't understand.

"Honey? Are you okay?" Stella asked, looking at Amanda with concern.

"Sure, sure," Amanda said, snapping out of her thoughts.

"Is it that guy with the psycho girlfriend?"

"She's not his girlfriend anymore," Amanda said.

"Really?" Stella smiled. "Good for you. And for him," she added, winking. "Do you two have a date?"

"No," Amanda said, wishing she hadn't revealed anything to her aunt. Stella was so outgoing, she couldn't understand what it was like to be shy. She always pushed Amanda to be more assertive than she was.

"Well, why not?" Stella asked. "You should call him—"

Just then there was a knock on the front window. Amanda looked up with great hope—

Tom?—only to see Stella's boyfriend, Antonio, waving at her.

Stella buttoned her coat. "Oh! Got to go. There's a birthday party for Louise—you want to come?" Stella had her hand on the door. "Wait—don't tell me. I can't stand more rejection." She smiled. "See you in the morning, sweetie."

"Good night, Aunt Stella." Amanda finished the accounts and went into the kitchen for a glass of milk. The little crab scuttled out of his pie dish of water and waved a claw at her. "You hungry?" she asked. She fed him a green bean, which she had discovered was his favorite food. "Should I forget about him?" she asked the crab. He waved a claw no—or at least to Amanda it looked that way.

"What am I doing, asking a crab for love advice? I'd better get some sleep." She went out the front door, and as she pulled the security gate down over the window, she noticed a man approaching. She whipped around. It was Tom. He was carrying flowers.

"Oh—hi," she said, trying not to seem too excited.

"Hi," he said. He looked at her—and couldn't stop looking, she was so beautiful in the moonlight.

"Something wrong?" she asked when he didn't say anything more.

"N-No, no, nothing, I just—" he stammered. He offered her the flowers.

"Vanilla orchids," Amanda said. "Where did you find them? You hardly ever see them." She inhaled their sweet vanilla scent and looked at Tom, who was smiling broadly. "What's so funny?"

"You . . . smelling those flowers. The way your nose crinkles—"

"—makes you laugh?" she asked.

"Makes me feel good," he answered.

Amanda's heart was beating so hard, she thought it might burst through her ribs. He looked so handsome—and here he was, bringing her flowers.

"Is there a place around here where we could grab a bite? Seeing you makes me want dessert for some reason," he said.

"How 'bout here?"

"I don't want you to go to any trouble—"

"It wouldn't be any trouble at all," she said. She hoisted up the gate.

Tom followed her inside the dark restaurant. He couldn't remember how he'd got there. One minute he was leaving his office, and the next he was grabbing the flowers off a perfume display and hailing a cab downtown. All on impulse.

Amanda led him into the kitchen and collected some ingredients from the shelves. "How was your meeting?" she asked.

Tom remembered he'd lied about his evening. Looking at Amanda's sweet, open face, he suddenly couldn't bring himself to lie again. "There was no meeting. I don't know why I pretended there was one. I don't know why I'm telling you this now. I'm sorry," he said.

"That's okay," she said. "I understand."

"You do?"

"I think so," she said simply. "You weren't sure you wanted to see me again, but you didn't want to hurt my feelings, so you made something up."

He watched as she turned up the heat under

a pot. "That sounds about right. The other day was so . . . *weird*, it kind of scared me."

"Me too," Amanda said. She stirred some cream into the pot.

Tom enjoyed seeing her at work. She was completely at ease in the kitchen. He liked just watching her, and stood closer.

He picked up the bouquet of vanilla orchids. "Hey, I should put these in some water."

Amanda looked up from the pot. "No, I have an idea. Bring them here," she said. As he passed the flowers to her, their hands touched and their eyes met. She took a flower stem and swirled it through the bubbling cream, then did the same with each of the rest. A vanilla-scented steam rose from the pot. Slowly Amanda rubbed the tiny flowers between her fingers until the petals broke off and dropped into the foaming white sauce. The steam grew thicker, the smell of flowers and vanilla mixing and filling the air, enveloping Tom and Amanda.

Her face was dewy from the vanilla fog, and Tom couldn't resist: He leaned over and kissed her cheek. "Mmmmm, you taste so good," he said.

She touched his face with her fingers. "You do too," she said.

Tom kissed her again, and the vanilla fog rolled out of the pot, wrapping them in its heavenly scent.

Eight

"*Ramos! Wait!*" Tom rushed over to one of his assistants. Tom had overslept but was in such high spirits he didn't mind a bit.

The assistant looked very worried. "Oh, Tom, I've been looking for you."

Tom swept his arm through the air. "Those orchids on the perfume display. The vanilla ones? We need more. I want them everywhere opening night," he said. He charged up the central staircase two steps at a time.

Ramos hurried to keep up with him. "But we already paid for two thousand roses—"

"I don't care," Tom said. "I want the whole place smelling like vanilla." He turned to Ramos. "Have you ever smelled those orchids? They're *amazing*. They're like a perfume that makes you feel great."

Ramos gazed at Tom, surprised he was suddenly so interested in flowers. "Okay, but, Tom, there's a problem. Valderon won't work."

"What?" Tom walked down the hall toward his office. "Why not?"

Ramos struggled to keep up. "The airline lost his knives."

Tom shrugged. "So get him some new ones. With what we're spending on the restaurant, a new set of—"

"He doesn't want new ones," Ramos interrupted. "He wants his own set."

Tom stopped and faced the assistant. "So get him the closest to his you can, and he'll get over it. Just take care of it, Ramos."

Entering his office, Tom found Jonathan sitting at his desk. Jonathan had never set foot inside his office before. Tom felt his stomach drop. "Good morning, Jonathan," he managed to say.

Jonathan stared Tom down. "It's not morning anymore, Tom. Morning was when we had a meeting with the bankers, oh, about two hours ago!"

Tom had completely forgotten about the quarterly meeting. How could he have forgotten? He was completely befuddled.

"We decided to go ahead without you," Jonathan continued, and shot a paper airplane toward the wastebasket. "Is this what you do in here all day? Play with paper airplanes?"

Behind Tom's desk was a row of his favorite planes. Jonathan continued to shoot them across the room one by one as he told Tom about a dream he'd had the night before. "In this dream, I was wearing a tuxedo, and I could see the reflection of my grandfather's face in my patent leather shoes. It was the opening of Jonathan's, and I was having a wonderful time."

"Great," Tom said, feeling some relief.

"Except!" Jonathan shot another paper plane across the room. It struck the wall, denting its nose, and fell to the carpet. "Every time I looked down at my shoes, my grandfather was sticking his tongue out at me. Why do you think he was doing that?"

The dream had turned into a nightmare. Tom said, "I really don't know."

Jonathan threw the last airplane. It too missed the wastebasket. He stood and tapped Tom's shoulder as he passed him on the way to the door. "It's disturbing me. I want you to keep thinking about it, because I know I will be." He left Tom's office.

Tom sighed and closed the office door, his jubilant mood from the night before gone. Tom had *never* missed a meeting. In the five years he'd worked at Bendel's, Jonathan had never doubted Tom or threatened him.

It was *Amanda*. She had upset his ordered life so quickly! Tom was afraid he shouldn't see her again until he got his life back under control. He dialed her number, intending to tell her just that. "Amanda?"

"Hi," she answered brightly. "It's so nice to hear from you. I didn't think I would so soon, I mean I'm glad—"

"I just wanted to say . . ." He pictured her smiling, the phone under her big mane of hair as she created some new, delicious entree.

"What?" she asked.

"That I had an amazing time last night," he said. "It was really fun, and . . . I can't wait to see you again."

"Me too," she said.

Tom heard a loud crash at her end of the line, then, "Whoops!" Amanda said. "I'd better go! The crab knocked over a bowl of egg whites! Talk to you later!"

"Okay . . . bye." Tom hung up, confused. He felt better after just hearing her voice, but hadn't he decided to break it off for a while? What was wrong with him?

His day passed that way. He felt as if he was in a fog—only not a sweet one like the night before. He coasted through his various meetings and the staff lunch, but he didn't feel as if he was really there. All he could think about was Amanda.

"We're worried about the startup costs," one of the German businessmen said.

Tom and the owners of a Berlin department store were standing in Jonathan's; Tom was showing them the restaurant in hopes that they would open a branch in Berlin.

"And all of this is dependent on Valderon, who is famous for being temperamental," another businessman said.

"That's true," Tom said. "But Valderon is contractually committed to creating the recipes and hiring the chefs, so you'll be getting Valderon's brilliance without his unpredictability." Suddenly Tom was distracted by a smell that was so heavenly he couldn't concentrate. The Germans stood waiting for him to continue.

"Now, about the startup expenses," Tom said, sniffing the air. "Many one-time-only costs"—he sniffed again—"like the fees for our *delicious* design, and our *mouthwatering* market research"—sniff, sniff—"and our *delectable* ad campaign"—sniff, sniff—"If you'll excuse me one moment . . ." He dashed away, a possessed man. The Germans watched him go, absolutely perplexed.

Tom ran down the stairs, following the smell. He stopped at one floor, sniffed, and continued down to the next, where he followed his nose to the scarf display. There two old people stood giggling, trying on scarves. They were Howard and Ruth from the Southern Cross Restaurant. Howard wrapped a scarf around Ruth's neck and kissed her sweetly. Tom watched them, overcome by the delicious smell that was literally driving him mad.

The couple moved on to the sunglasses counter, trying on the most outrageous pairs they could find and laughing. They were having a ball together, like young lovers. Tom could wait no longer. He stepped in front of them, startling them. "Excuse me!" he said in his most officious voice. "Are you carrying—food?"

Howard stepped away. "Why, yes, but—"

Ruth opened her bag. Nestled inside was that familiar pink box from the Southern Cross.

Tom grabbed it, outraged. "I'm sorry, but I must confiscate this! We have a new policy. No outside food. Due to the rats!" And he ran off with the box, leaving behind a most bewildered Ruth and Howard.

Safely inside his office, Tom placed his prized quarry on the desk and lovingly opened it. A half-eaten caramel éclair was in the box. A little disappointing, but the smell reminded him of the feeling he'd soon be having if he took just one bite. He stepped into his closet, where he kept silverware and plates. When he came out, he saw Lois standing over his desk, finishing off the éclair!

"Nooooo!" he screamed.

"You've got to learn to share, Tom," she said. "This is really good. Actually, this is *incredible* . . ." A big smile spread across her face. "Got any more?" she asked breathlessly as the éclair took its effect on her. "Man, that was good. . . . *Wow.*" She slid into a chair, a dreamy look in her eye. "I wish Jonathan was around. I'd really like to . . . talk to him. Or something. Where'd you get that thing?"

Tom glared at her. "Where?" he said, becoming completely undone. "I'll tell you where! I mugged a seventy-five-year old lady for it! I'm losing it, Lois. Big-time. And right when Jonathan's having those Grandfather-from-beyond-the-grave dreams again." Tom held his head in his hands. "I can't stop thinking about her! We made out on a vanilla cloud!"

"A vanilla cloud? In New York?"

Tom leaned on his desk. "This girl, she's amazing, Lois. She's beautiful and funny and sweet and she can cook things that make you *crazy*! It's chaos, Lois. A bit early, it's only our second date, but what a date it was. More like a third. Actually, it was off the charts, like a lifetime of amazing dates," he said forlornly. He felt weak.

Lois knew what was coming next: Tom was going to say he shouldn't see her again.

"I shouldn't see her again," Tom stated definitively. "That's the answer."

Lois stifled a laugh. He was falling in love with this girl, that was obvious. If she encouraged him to see her, he'd only resist harder. She decided to play it differently. "You're right. This *is* it, Tom. You'd better run. Especially now. You don't have time for this." Lois tried to sound serious.

Tom pounded a fist on the desk. "I know! Look at me! Chasing pastry! I don't even *eat* dessert!"

Lois put a frown on her face. "You're a wreck. She's got you all tangled up in your underwear. Whatever you do, don't ever see her again."

"Absolutely not." Tom nodded. "I can't." He

loved spending time with Amanda, but he just *should not* see her again. Not until the restaurant opened and he was more in control of his life. He didn't want to hurt her, though. She would understand if he simply and nicely explained his feelings to her. "I'll just go down there and tell her—"

Lois took his arm. "Go down there? Are you crazy? It's *way* too risky. Use the phone, Tom," she instructed, seeing that he was determined to see Amanda again. All he needed was to be dared not to, and he'd be sure to go.

"I do this all the time, Lois," he argued. "I know what I'm doing."

"Not this time."

Tom brushed her off. "You think I'll succumb to her, don't you? You think I'll weaken once I see her beautiful face and hear that voice."

"You can't handle it," Lois said, playing it straight.

"*You* think I can't handle it."

"You *can't*," Lois insisted.

"Oh, *please*," Tom said, annoyed. "Just to prove it to you, I'll go down there and calmly have a little bite, something light and simple and quick, and tell her. She's a wonderful girl, Lois. She'll understand. No big deal. You watch."

"It'll be my pleasure," Lois said, already feeling victorious. "But first, you might want to finish your meeting with the Germans." She pointed toward the door, where the businessmen were waiting.

Tom strode around his desk, brushing a hand down his lapel. "Ah, yes! Mr. Mueller, sorry to keep you." He led the men from his office.

Lois gazed at the empty pink box on Tom's desk and leaned down, inhaling deeply. She *had* to have some more of those éclairs. They might just be the key that would unlock Jonathan's heart. There was something magical about them. Lois was sure Jonathan liked her but was just too shy to express it. She'd tried every other way to reach him—why not try food? Didn't someone once say that the way to a man's heart was through his stomach? If ever there was a food that could do the trick, Lois thought, it was one of those éclairs.

She called her secretary. "Annie? When's my

meeting with Jonathan? . . . *Great*. That'll give you enough time to get downtown and buy some pastries. . . . Yes, pastries. I'll tell you later, or hopefully, I won't need to. . . . You'll see why yourself. Now, the place is called the Southern Cross, and I want as many caramel éclairs as they have. . . . And hurry."

Nine

Amanda was cooking like the four-star chef she had once only dreamed of being. Rack of lamb and filet of sole; curried shrimp and chili-dusted duck; gnocchi and risotto; Thai-style noodle dishes; every kind of vegetable!

But Amanda felt her real specialty was desserts. During the morning hours and in the afternoons between lunch and dinner, she prepared all kinds of sweets. The treats ranged from her now-famous caramel éclairs to raspberry tarts to chocolate soufflés. With love she stirred and poured and folded, and she believed that love was the secret ingredient that made the food taste so good, and made the people who ate it feel so good.

Her life had changed so fast, and all because of one person. Tom had brought out the best in her, and she gave it back to everyone who tasted her cooking. They hadn't even spent that much time together, but Amanda felt as if she truly *knew* him, and she knew she wanted to get to know him even better. As she glazed a crème brûlée she marveled at the power of love, at how inexplicable it was, how fast it could change your whole life. And the only time she wasn't happy was when she worried that it might end. But why would it? Tom seemed as infatuated as she was. He'd called that very morning just to tell her that. She told herself she had nothing to worry about—everything was great between them—and she began to make her signature dessert, caramel éclairs.

Tom worked late, trying to make up for all the goofs he'd made that day. He read the minutes of the bankers' meeting he had missed, then drafted some memos and letters based on what had happened there. The departmental budgets needed to be reviewed, and as he opened the big binder for the cosmetics department, that sweet smell from the éclairs drifted under his nose. He shook his head and tried to concentrate on the rows of numbers. But that smell—where was it coming from? He must be imagining it. *I'm really losing it*, he thought. *Now I'm having scent hallucinations*.

Meanwhile, down in the lobby, Lois was waiting for an elevator. One was out of service, which left only one for the whole store. Tom was really slipping—that would *never* have happened before he became involved with this young woman. It was great to see someone who was usually so buttoned down become so rattled. She only hoped her friend would let himself go with what he felt and not fight his feelings for Amanda.

As for herself, Lois hoped the little box of éclairs she held in her hands would do to Jonathan what they had done for Tom. Now, if she could only get him to eat just one . . .

Ping!

The doors opened and she stepped on. The elevator stopped on the very next floor, and to her delight, Jonathan stepped into the small elevator.

"Hello, Lois," he said shyly. He always seemed slightly embarrassed with her, which

Lois found charming. It made her want to relax him. Jonathan sniffed, looked at the pink box. "Smells good. What is it?"

With great finesse and a big smile, Lois slowly lifted the lid. "Just a little treat for our meeting," she said.

The smell was so enticing, Jonathan couldn't resist. "Why wait?" he asked, and he grabbed one of the éclairs.

"My sentiments exactly," Lois said, and she bit into one too, watching Jonathan closely. He nodded approval, finishing the pastry off in two bites. "Mmmm . . . incredible . . . mmm," he said. He reached for another as the elevator made its slow ascent.

Back in his office, Tom was finding it hard to work. The vanilla smell was distracting, even though he told himself it was just his imagination.

There was no point in trying to work if he wasn't actually going to get anything done. He might as well leave and come in early the next morning, when he'd cleared his head.

He stood at the elevator bank, waiting. The elevator seemed to be stuck on the fourth floor. He pressed and pressed the button, even though he knew it would have no effect. With one elevator out of service, he had to wait for this one or walk down eight flights. "Come on, come on," he muttered, suddenly impatient to see Amanda. He reminded himself that he was going down to the restaurant to break it off—just for a little while—and that he must stick to that plan, no matter how wonderful she looked or felt or . . .

Ping!

The elevator doors opened at last. Inside, Jonathan and Lois were locked in an embrace, oblivious to the world around them. Tom cleared his throat. Still they didn't stop kissing. The elevator doors started to close, and Tom took a step forward, noticing the telltale empty pink pastry box on the floor. Jonathan casually backed away from Lois, took her hand, and escorted her off the elevator.

As she passed Tom, she smiled a devilish smile and licked her lips. "I knew it!" she whispered. "He's *crazy* about me!" Tom smiled, happy for both of them.

Amanda's cooking sure was powerful.

It was mayhem. Every surface in the kitchen was covered with food or plates waiting to be served or filled with food. In the center of all this, Amanda whirled and chopped and sautéed, while Nolan tried to keep up with her. They had brought back Youssef, the old Pakistani waiter, to help serve, and with Stella working the bar and serving food, the Southern Cross was up and running again. It was already past ten at night, and the place was still busy.

"Amanda, you have a guest," Stella said, entering the kitchen with Tom behind her.

Stella picked up a couple of plates, passing one to Tom to hold while she picked up another. "I hesitate to give you another of these, but would you mind? Just hold this for a sec. Try not to throw it." She handed him a second plate, then was gone, leaving Tom holding the two dinners.

Amanda was thrilled to see him, but between grilling a sea bass and roasting a game hen and the six sizzling pans of various vegetables, she couldn't stop to give him a kiss. "This is great!" she said. "I didn't expect to see you tonight."

He stammered, "W-Well, we need . . . I need to talk to you. But I think I should come back—"

"Would you mind holding this?" She shoved another plate at him. He adjusted the first two and took the third. There wasn't a single surface to set the plates on.

"You look great!" she said, giving him a quick kiss.

Nolan cleared his throat. "This must be Tom," he said, taking one plate off Tom's arm and replacing it with another. "Nice to meet you," he said.

"Nice to meet you," Tom replied.

"I've heard so much about you, I feel like I already know you," Nolan said.

Tom squirmed. He didn't like the idea of someone talking about him. "Great, great. It's good to be . . . known."

Amanda read the uneasy expression on Tom's face. "Nolan meant about the store, and the restaurant you're opening. Didn't you, Nolan?"

Nolan garnished a platter. "And how you like to make paper airplanes and how sweet you are even though you try to hide it—"

"*Nolan*, where are the artichokes?" Amanda interrupted.

Youssef entered and took two plates off Tom's arms and passed back through the kitchen doors. Nolan laid another plate on Tom's arm and whispered, "She's nuts about you, man."

And I'm nuts about her, Tom thought. *I'd have to be, to be standing here like a human counter.* "Maybe there's a better way I can help here," he said. "There must be a way I can organize this place. . . ." For a moment the kitchen traffic slowed enough for him to do just that. He lined up the completed plates in a row, their paper orders beneath them, and when Youssef or Stella came in with new orders, he shouted them to Amanda. A system was born. The cramped kitchen quickly became less chaotic.

"Table two wants—" Tom yelled.

"Don't tell me, let me guess," Amanda said.

"How could you?" Tom wondered.

"I saw them come in. Grilled tuna for her, the lamb for him?" she asked.

Tom looked at the order in his hands. "How did you know—are they regulars?"

Amanda shrugged. "I've never seen them before. I can tell they're on a date. She's wearing too much makeup, and his shoes are polished. So they ordered *date* food. She orders something light and inexpensive so she won't look like a pig; he wants the beef but orders the lamb, not wanting to seem too macho."

Tom was impressed. "I guess you've been doing this awhile," he said. "Can you predict what I'd like to eat tonight?"

Amanda arranged a pile of vegetables on a side plate. "No. Nothing about you is predictable," she laughed.

At the end of the evening, Amanda placed a tablecloth and candle on the stainless steel counter so that Tom could eat while she cooked and finished cleaning up. There was a towering pile of dirty dishes in the sink. "I guess it's time to hire a dishwasher," she said.

"You don't have one?" Tom asked.

"Until recently, we didn't need one," she explained. "Nolan, Stella, and I managed to do everything."

Tom took a bite of his fish. "That seems impossible. The place is absolutely packed."

"*That's* what seems impossible," Amanda said. "It used to be dead."

"But you're such an amazing cook," he said.

"Suddenly. Like almost miraculously," Amanda said, wondering if she could confide in Tom about all the strange things that had been happening lately. She didn't understand them, and maybe they were all just coincidences, but there was no denying that something incredible was going on.

"It's like a lot of things," Tom said between bites of his food. "You try and try and try, and just when you're about to throw in the towel, everything comes together for you. Like when you learn to ride a bike. You fall down nine times in a row, and then the tenth time, you ride for a mile."

Amanda admitted it did make sense—there were some things that finally just clicked into place. As she gazed at the counter and thought about this, a leaf of lettuce gently floated across the counter of its own accord. Amanda's eyes popped. How could anyone explain *that*?

Tom calmly lifted the lettuce leaf to reveal the little crab underneath. "You again!" Tom looked at Amanda, amused. "What is he, your pet?"

"He seems to have adopted me," Amanda said cheerfully. "I can't blame him for not wanting to be your crab napoleon."

"Just what I was craving," Tom said jokingly, reaching for the crab. He scuttled away.

"How about some dessert instead?" Amanda asked.

"Sure!"

She placed a basket of fresh fruit on the counter. She held a peach in her hand and began to cut it with a knife. Then the knife seemed to take over, and the peach turned in her hands, a tendril of soft skin very slowly spiraling down in one long, perfect strand. It was beautiful.

Tom watched, spellbound. "That's a very, very good knife," he said.

"You think that's what it is?" she asked.

"A very impressive aerodynamic phenomenon," Tom explained.

"Like the way a paper airplane can fly."

"That *is* fun, isn't it?"

Amanda decided it was time to ask him something she'd been wanting to ask since it had happened that afternoon in Jonathan's restaurant. "And the band?"

Tom seemed nonplussed. "It was a hallucination."

Amanda pressed him. "We both had the same one?"

"It was a sugar rush from the éclairs," he said, trying to rationalize it. "And there we were, on that dance floor, alone. We were swept away by our imaginations, is all."

Amanda wasn't convinced these things could be so easily explained away. Something weird was going on, and it couldn't be just because

New York needed another good restaurant. She placed the peach slices in a pan of melting butter, added cinnamon and sugar, and sautéed the mixture. Tom saw that she was still worried. He came over to her and gently swept the hair back from her cheeks.

"The band was like déjà vu—really vivid, but not really real." He plucked a slice of peach from the pan and ate it, staring into her eyes. "*Everything* seems that way to me now, everything tastes better and looks better, and it's all because of you," he said, kissing her. He took the spoon from her hand and licked it, and then he kissed her. The spoon fell from his hand but floated, ever so gracefully, to the floor. As they kissed more passionately, they slowly started floating off the floor.

"I love kissing you," Tom said.

"I love you too," Amanda said. When Tom heard those words, his eyes popped open—something about those three words made him nervous. And then he realized he had real reason to be scared: He was six feet off the ground, floating near the ceiling of the kitchen!

"Whooaaa!" he cried.

Amanda looked around and giggled. It was wild! They were floating, like in *Mary Poppins*.

Tom was panicking. "What's happening? What's going on?"

"We're floating!" Amanda shrieked, delighted.

Tom was horrified. "Well, stop it! Do something!"

"It's amazing," Amanda said, trying to "swim" a little.

"No, it isn't! This sucks!" he yelped.

Amanda was disappointed that Tom wasn't enjoying it. She floated gently to the floor. But Tom remained six feet above her head.

"Why can't I get down?" he asked, frightened.

"Don't get hysterical," she told him.

"I'm not hysterical! I'm trapped!" He pushed off the ceiling, hoping to reach the floor, but he bounced back up like an apple in a bucket of water. "You did this to me . . . now undo it."

Amanda balked. *"What?* I didn't *do* anything, so how would I know how to undo it?"

"Figure it out!" he called.

Amanda was shocked that Tom was so upset—and that he was stuck up there. She thought maybe if she could make him laugh, he would relax and float down. "Okay, the undo secret," she said. She jokingly wiggled her nose. "Bibbity, bobbity *boo*!"

He didn't laugh. "Real funny. Just leave me alone. I'll figure it out myself," he said miserably.

"Fine," Amanda said. She left the kitchen. At the bar she waited and worried. How *had* it happened? A loud crash interrupted her thoughts. She ran into the kitchen to find Tom under a heap of pots and pans on the floor. He stood up, seeming angry and afraid at the same time.

"Say something," Amanda said after a long silence.

He gave her a cold look. "I'd better go," he said.

"What?" she asked.

He looked at her distantly, evaluating her. "I knew I shouldn't see you again," he said.

Amanda was stunned. Why would he feel that way? She thought about it for a moment, and then it dawned on her. "You're afraid of me," she said.

Tom nodded. "Hell, *yes*! I kiss you and then you pin me to the ceiling. . . . And *you* think it's funny! I'm not sticking around to find out what else you can do to me."

Amanda put her hands on her hips. "You didn't seem to mind making out in a vanilla fog last night—"

He took a step away from her. "You made me do that," he declared. "You tricked me."

"I did not!" she said. "It just happened!"

He crossed his arms over his chest. "*Precisely!* Whenever I'm around you things 'just happen' and you're the one calling the shots. You're some kind of a witch, and I'm a mere man."

"Mere is right," Amanda said, tears stinging her eyes.

He wagged a finger at her. "Don't twist this around," he said. "I'm not some jerk who won't give up his Tuesday-night poker game or something. This is not about compromising or being flexible— it's about my free will! Who knows what else you could do? I have to be in control of my destiny."

His words sounded like something he'd read in a self-help book. Amanda couldn't believe he meant them. "Your destiny?" she asked incredulously. "You bumped your head on the ceiling! You can't be serious." She hoped she'd get through to the Tom she knew and loved. Who was this freaked-out guy standing before her?

"I couldn't be more serious," Tom said. He turned away and walked out of the kitchen and into the dining room.

Amanda followed him. "Well then, you're in trouble," she warned him. "A man's character *is* his destiny."

Tom stood in the doorway and turned back, giving her a hard look. "That's *right*! *Exactly*." He stopped, a thought crossing his mind. "Wait— *what*? What's that? Is that supposed to be some kind of curse?"

Amanda gave him a shove out the door and slammed and locked it behind him. "In your case it is!" she screamed through the glass. She turned her back to him, wiping away her angry tears. *What a jerk!* she thought. *How could I ever have even liked someone like him?* He obviously didn't like her anyway, so she should just get over it and forget all about Mr. Tom Bartlett.

CHAPTER Ten

Rain poured from the sky.

Tom stormed down the street, searching for a cab. It was very late, *and* it was pouring. She was probably behind the weather too, he thought. After walking for about ten blocks, he was finally able to flag down an empty cab. He waved it over, and as it reached the curb, it hit a deep puddle, splashing him from head to toe.

"Seventy-third and Lexington," he said, plucking at his wet pants. *What a night,* he thought. *She levitated me!* He knew she was a talented, interesting woman, but that was too much! He shuddered just thinking about the things she could do, especially if she got mad. Then he realized that Amanda *was* mad. Hadn't she cursed him? Who knew what might happen now? He shivered and hugged himself for warmth. Feeling his jacket, he noticed the absence of his wallet from his breast pocket. He patted his other pockets, but located no wallet. *It's already happening,* he thought. *She stole my wallet!*

"Uh, sir, listen, I seem to have lost my wallet," he said to the cabdriver. "But if you wait out front I think I'll be able to dig up enough cash—" The cab screeched to a halt and the driver leapt up from his seat, hauled Tom out of the cab, and dumped him on the sidewalk in a heap.

"Hey!" was all Tom managed to say before the taxi sped away.

And then he heard a low growl. He looked up to see a large, angry gray dog baring its teeth at him.

Tom slowly backed away from the dog, but the dog started after him. Tom picked up speed, and so did the dog. Tom began to trot, throwing glances back over his shoulder. The dog matched his pace. Tom broke into a run, still looking over his shoulder. The dog was gaining, howling and drooling . . . and then, *ripppp!* The dog took a bite out of Tom's pants and—

Thwonk!

Tom ran smack into a lamppost.

The dog yelped at the noise and ran off.

Tom held his head, dazed. Rain fell over his face. "This is unbelievable," he muttered. At least the dog was gone. Now if only it would stop pouring.

The dog had chased Tom down one of Manhattan's more obscure streets. Tom saw a blinking store sign up ahead and decided to stop in to wait until the rain let up.

The sign read THE THIRD EYE and beneath that, HOURS: MIDNIGHT TILL 8 AM. *Only in New York*, Tom thought. He stepped inside, happy to be in a dry place, barely noticing the window display of black candles, crystals, magic books, and other occult paraphernalia.

He was browsing the bookshelf just inside the door when the salesman approached him. He was a very tall man, nearly seven feet tall, with one blue eye and one brown, and long matted dreadlocks.

"You must be in trouble," he said to Tom.

Tom nearly jumped out of his skin. "How can you tell?"

"Well, the big blue bruise on your forehead,

for one," the man drawled in an accent Tom couldn't place. "And you don't look like our usual customers, for two. And for three—that's the self-help section you're in."

Tom looked at the man, then around the store, and then at the row of titles on the shelf: *Good Witches Who Love Bad Mortals*, *Bad Warlocks Who Love Good Mortals*, *What to Do When Your Powers Start Fading*, *300 Common Curses and How to Undo Them*. He was in an occult store! What were the chances of that happening? He started laughing hysterically— Amanda's powers were stronger than he'd imagined.

The salesman continued to stare. "Yep. It's *big* trouble. You want to tell me about it? Maybe I can help."

Tom started telling the man about his strange days with Amanda. The man convinced Tom that the answer was to hold a scepter while standing in a pentagram of salt. Wet, scared, desperate, and tired, Tom agreed it might be a good solution.

"So besides the ceiling thing, what else has

been happening?" the salesman asked Tom, carefully shaking salt across the floor from a large carton.

Tom shoved his hands into his pockets. "I've been very confused and . . . disoriented. Missing appointments, changing my mind, that kind of thing."

"Yes. What else?" the man asked, circling Tom.

"I saw an apparition. A band. In tuxedos."

"Were their eyes red?"

Tom was baffled by the question but answered, "No."

"What were they playing?"

"These Foolish Things."

The man stopped circling Tom. "Come on, man. Give me something to work with here."

"A mean gray dog came after me and—"

"A hellhound—"

"Yes!" Tom exclaimed. "A *hellhound* chased me into a lamppost!"

"Now we're getting somewhere," the man said, excited.

"I got thrown out of a cab because—now, get

this! I couldn't find my wallet, and that's never, never happened to me!"

The man looked up at Tom sharply. "You don't have your wallet? No checkbook?"

Before Tom could say *"Shazzam!"* he found himself thrown out onto the street. "We're not a charity, buddy!" the salesman said, slamming the door.

Tom stood and started walking uptown to his apartment. What a nightmare! At least it had stopped raining. He walked and walked and walked. More than thirty blocks, and at last he reached his building. There was a new doorman on duty. Tom nodded to him and tried to walk to the elevator, but the doorman stopped him.

"And you're here to see?" the doorman asked.

"My apartment, thank you. I live here. Who are you? Where's Joe?"

"Joe is off tonight, sir. I'm afraid I'll have to see some ID. You understand. Security."

This was too much. How had Amanda done it? How had she gotten this all organized so fast? Tom sighed and smiled at the doorman. "I have had a really bad night, one component of which involved losing my wallet, so I have no ID on me. Now, I just walked over thirty blocks in the rain, and I'm going into my apartment."

"I can't allow that, sir—"

Tom grabbed the doorman's lapels and snapped, "Do I look like someone who doesn't live here? Do I?"

"Well, yes, you look rather . . . disheveled, sir," the doorman replied.

Tom calmed down and proposed an idea. He still had his keys, so he would use them to get in and then show the doorman his passport or something. The doorman agreed to the proposal.

As Tom laid his head on his pillow, he reviewed the night's events. He found that his feelings for Amanda were so strong that even now, even after this night of hell, he wished he could see her. *I'm under her spell*, he thought. *No wonder all I can think of is her.* But how did she do it? Tom didn't really believe in witches, but there was definitely something supernatural going on. Ever since lunch that day . . .

And then it hit him. She must be a *food*

witch who made things happen through her cooking. He started recalling all the food-induced events of the past couple of weeks: After eating the éclair, he'd danced and imagined he saw and heard a band! And look what had happened to Lois and Jonathan after just a few bites. And tonight, all it took was a lick of that spoon and he was floating off the ground.

It was incredible, but it seemed to be true. At least he'd figured out how she did it. It gave him some comfort to understand the phenomenon. Now all he was worried about was how long the curse would last.

And what further havoc it might bring.

CHAPTER

Eleven

It was dawn. Amanda stood on the Brooklyn Bridge as she had done so many times before and looked out at the harbor, the Statue of Liberty, and, of course, the majestic skyline of New York City. Spring air, sweet and warm, blew through her hair, and she remembered the morning she'd tossed her coin here and, later, spotted Tom at the market.

It all felt like so long ago. Now Tom was afraid of her—and worse, he believed she was some kind of witch! She knew things had been weird lately, but she also knew she couldn't just "make" things happen. Besides, if she could, she would never do anything to hurt him. Amanda believed that the magic happened *because* of him, that the combination of Tom and Amanda caused incredible events. Why wouldn't he want to find out what more they could do together? *If being in control is more important than being in love*, Amanda thought, *then fine, he can have his control*. She marched down the boardwalk into Manhattan. Like a pinball, her feelings had bounced all night from anger to disappointment to yearning.

Stella was waiting for her on a bench at the Union Square market, reading the paper and drinking a cup of coffee. She smiled at Amanda and handed her a folded section of the newspaper. "Look! Look!" she said excitedly.

Amanda read the headline, "TriBeCa Gem Rediscovered: Magic in the Kitchen," and scanned the glowing review. Now the Southern Cross would *really* get busy. She handed the paper back to Stella.

"With a review like that I think we just might make it, sweetie," Stella said. "Miracles really do happen." She shook her head, amazed at the reversal in the Southern Cross's fortunes. "Why aren't you more excited?" she asked her niece.

Amanda's face was stony. "I am, I am."

"No, you're not. What's wrong? You look terrible."

Amanda sighed and watched the market come alive. Tears filled her eyes. She tried to get mad again, but she couldn't help it. She loved Tom and already missed him. She couldn't believe he really didn't want her anymore. "Tom and I broke up last night. We were kissing, and then . . . then we started floating," she said simply. There was no other way of putting it, and if she couldn't tell Stella, whom could she tell?

"Metaphorically?" Stella asked.

"No. *Literally*. And he completely freaked out. Like it was something horrible."

"You mean, off-the-ground floating?" Stella asked, disbelieving.

"Yeah."

"Well . . ." Stella sighed, trying to figure this out. She wasn't particularly interested in the supernatural, but she wasn't a skeptic either. Anything was possible. Of course, maybe Amanda and Tom had just *felt* as if they were floating, and felt it so strongly that they actually believed it had happened. Either way, the problem was that Tom didn't like it. "He's probably never floated before," Stella said, unsure of what advice to give. "You know, men generally have a hard time with new experiences. . . ."

Amanda slumped down on the bench. "What should I do? You know more about this stuff than I do."

"I do?" Stella asked, confounded. "I've had some good times, but I don't think I've ever floated, sweetie."

"I don't mean that. I mean with men."

"Oh, men . . ." Stella sighed. "Knowing many men doesn't mean I've learned anything. I've just been confused longer. But let's see . . . about this guy, Tom. It sounds like he's scared."

"Definitely," Amanda said.

"He seems like the type who likes to control everything. His sock drawer is probably very organized. So being with you . . ." Stella paused.

"Would mess up his sock drawer?" Amanda replied.

"Among other things, yes. Do you think he loves you, Amanda?"

"I thought he did."

Stella folded up the newspaper. "Here's something I have learned. When it comes to love, there seem to be two types of people in the world: those who love falling in love, and those who prefer *being* loved. That's the day-in, day-out type, like Ruth and Howard. I'm the other type, who likes the falling part, when everyone's on their best behavior and everything is real romantic. When things get a little bumpy, I run. I'm not so good at the staying there part."

Amanda loved her aunt so much, she wanted a wonderful man to love Stella too, and take care of her. She couldn't believe that Stella didn't want that herself. "Maybe you should give it a try," she said. "Maybe you'd find out *being* loved is even better."

"That's what Antonio keeps telling me," Stella said casually. "He asked me to marry him yesterday."

Amanda was amazed. "That's wonderful!"

Stella waved a hand, dismissing the proposal. "Sure, sure . . . Listen, sweetie, I'm *sixty-five*. I know what I'm good at and what I'm not good at by now. And I wouldn't be good at marriage."

"Tom sounds like you. The minute things got

a little shaky, he ran. I guess I'd better forget about him."

"No, no," Stella said. "He does sound like my type, but my type at his age could turn into your type with some help."

Amanda was completely confused now. "What do you mean?"

Stella crossed her legs. "You have to show him *being* in love is even better than *falling* in love. If I had crossed paths with someone like you, somebody so stubborn and so loving, I could have turned into the other type."

Amanda chewed nervously on her bottom lip. "He's probably too mad."

Stella patted her niece's arm. "If you don't give him one more chance, you'll be depriving yourself of the chance too. And *that* I don't want to see. Talk to him. Tell him how you feel. Then you'll know you did everything you could."

Amanda considered her aunt's advice. She didn't really like the idea of telling Tom how she felt, knowing he probably didn't want to hear it and would just reject her again. But if giving him one last chance would give *them* another chance, she'd risk the humiliation. Because being with Tom again was worth it. "I guess I could return his wallet," she said.

"You stole his wallet!" Stella laughed. "No wonder he's mad at you!"

"No, he dropped it last night. I found it on the kitchen floor."

"Honey, that's the oldest trick in the book," Stella said. She threw her arms around her niece. They stood up and walked toward the market stalls to shop for the day's produce.

Charlie and Abe waved them over. "We heard the good news," Charlie said. "Congratulations, Amanda."

"Your mother would be real proud of you," Abe said. "We're going to come down for lunch one of these days, see for ourselves."

"Thanks. I'd like that," Amanda said.

"And maybe we could go to the movies or something sometime," Charlie said.

This time Stella bailed her out. "It'd have to be a short film," she said. "This girl's busy these days. You don't think it's me that turned the place around, do you?" She laughed.

The other vendors had heard about the miraculous change and congratulated Amanda. "And I hear they're all your own recipes," Mr. Verini said. "That must have been the secret, huh? So try some Fuji apples, okay? You could whip up something magical, I bet." He winked.

Stella wanted to meet Gene, the man who'd sold Amanda the crabs, but he wasn't to be found. They asked around, but no one at the market had ever seen a man there selling crabs.

"That's strange, isn't it?" Amanda said.

"Compared to floating to the ceiling? I don't know. . . ." Stella raised her arm to hail a cab. "Where are you going?" she asked her niece.

Amanda looked at Stella, curious. "Home with you, to prep for lunch. Where else would I be going?"

"*Uptown*," Stella reminded her. "There's no time like the present."

"Oh, I don't know . . . ," Amanda hedged. She wasn't sure yet if this was the best thing to do. Maybe she should just leave Tom alone for a few days. Just leave him a message about his wallet.

A cab pulled over, and Stella held the door open for her niece. "You'll only be miserable until you talk to him. And that might make for some miserable food, miserable customers, miserable aunt, a whole long list of miserableness."

Amanda knew Stella was right. And besides, she didn't think she could wait much longer to see Tom again. She gave her aunt a peck on the cheek and slid into the back of the cab.

Twelve

Lois sailed down the hall, lighter than air. Ever since that night in the elevator, her life had been like a dream, with Jonathan in her arms at last. She'd *known* he liked her! He confessed that he always had but hadn't wanted to put her in an uncomfortable situation, since they worked together. Lois loved him all the more for being so thoughtful. She was worried that those éclairs might have been laced with some kind of sweet aphrodisiac and that Jonathan would realize he didn't want her, but so far, that didn't seem to be the case. Everything in her life was suddenly as sweet as those pastries.

Tom's secretary had stepped away from the office, and his door was closed, which was unusual. Lois tried the doorknob. She knocked. Eventually Tom opened the door a tiny crack and peered out. "Tom . . . ?" she asked.

Tom silently let her in and walked back to his desk.

The room was stifling. Tom's face was red, and lines creased his face. He appeared to be distracted with worry. Lois looked at him with concern. "Can I open a window?"

"No! She'll get in!" Tom screamed.

"*What*? Who'll get in?" she asked.

"*Amanda*," he whispered, afraid she might hear. "She's a witch!"

Lois stared at Tom. He'd lost it. From the look in his eyes, she knew he wasn't kidding around. It was only nine in the morning. Tom looked like a man who'd been up all night, his shirt wrinkled, his hair a mess. He hadn't shaved. This was not the Tom Lois had known for five years. Then she remembered her challenge to him—that he go down to the Southern Cross and not weaken at the sight of his beloved Amanda. From the look of things, he'd taken the dare.

Lois clapped her hands, jubilant. "*Bravo!* You succumbed! I knew it! You didn't break it off with her, did you?"

Tom flopped down in his desk chair. "I never had a chance. She pinned me to the ceiling."

"Really? How?"

Tom shook his head wearily. "I don't know. She put something in the food. And then she cursed me. She said in this really creepy voice, 'A man's character is his destiny.'"

Lois tapped a finger on her forehead, amused. "Oh, *right*, she's a wise witch. Casts her spells in proverbs."

Tom realized Lois didn't believe him, that she didn't understand what had happened. "I know you think I'm insane, Lois—"

"It's that old black magic . . ." She started humming the song.

"Lois, please—"

"It's got you in its spell . . . ," she sang.

"Lois!" he cried impatiently.

She leaned across his desk and stared into his eyes. "You're in love," she told him. "And *that* is *that*." The room was silent. Tom looked like a deer caught in headlights. He knew what she said was true.

He stammered, "If—If I'd just followed the rule, no fourth dates—"

Lois couldn't bear to hear any more of Tom's ridiculous rules and theories. "Here's _my_ rule," she said. "Live it up, and give it back—" She stopped because Tom was looking terrified suddenly. She turned around to see Amanda standing in the doorway.

"How did you get in here?" Tom asked her.

Amanda resisted the urge to run from the office. "Uh, the door. It was open," she answered, puzzled. Lois and Tom said nothing. The room was still. Amanda took a step into the room, and Tom leaned back in his chair.

Amanda laid his wallet on the desk. "I wanted to return this to you. You dropped it last night."

Lois offered her hand. "I take it you're Amanda," she said. "It's very nice to meet you. I'm Lois. And I was just leaving." She shook Amanda's hand and backed toward the door.

"No," Tom said to Lois, scared. "You stay."

Lois didn't like the idea but had to respect her friend's wishes. "Okay, if that's the way you want it." She looked at Amanda and shrugged. "Sorry."

"It's all right." Amanda looked at Tom. She tried to see whether there was still love in his eyes, but he looked so jumpy she wasn't sure. She took a deep breath and began the speech she'd prepared on the way uptown. "I know the last few weeks have been—odd."

"To say the least!" Tom agreed.

"All right, 'to say the least,'" Amanda conceded. "My whole life was ordinary, and then we met and these amazing things started to happen. I can't explain them, and I know that bothers you, and I can understand that. But I'm feeling like I could do . . . anything right now, and I don't know if I need you to keep that feeling, but . . . I know I want you."

Tom was stunned by Amanda's honest emotion. She was an amazing girl, and he was a stupid idiot coward. Still, he hesitated; she had these odd powers. . . . He wasn't sure he could ever handle being with her. He didn't want to lead her on, but he didn't want to lose her either.

"Uh, well . . . I don't know what to say. . . . I think . . . I don't know what to say," he repeated.

Lois wanted to kick him or slap some sense into him, but she kept still and watched.

Amanda tried to draw him out. "Well, how do you feel?"

He leaned forward over his desk, frustrated. "I feel . . . I feel . . . like I don't know."

Dead silence blanketed the room. And then, suddenly, a knife flew into the office, zipped past Tom's head, and stuck in the wall—followed by another. And then Chef Michel Valderon charged into the room.

Valderon's face was red with anger; with one hand he waved a third large knife. "*Voilà!* This is no knife!" He threw it, and Tom ducked. The knife hit the wall and stuck. "I spit on your American knife!" Valderon cried. And he did. He went around to each knife and spit on it. Valderon saw a menu from Jonathan's on Tom's desk and picked it up. "I spit on your restaurant!" And then he approached Tom. "And finally, I spit on—"

"No, no, allow me!" Tom yelled, and he spit on his own arm.

Valderon seemed impressed. "*That* were the first intelligent thing that you do! And now, I fire you!" he said in his poor English.

"You can't fire me!" Tom exclaimed.

Valderon marched to the door. "*Au revoir,* butthead."

Tom stood, outraged. "You can't leave! You're under contract!" But Valderon kept right on going.

Looking at Lois, Tom pointed at Amanda. "*See?* Now do you believe me? I told you she was a witch."

Amanda jumped in. "Wait a minute, you can't think I had something to do with this?"

"If the shoe fits, or should I say *broom?*" Tom said accusingly.

Amanda looked at him, furious. "That's ridiculous! How could I have made him do anything? He's crazy all by himself, anybody can see that. And why would I? You think—"

At that moment Jonathan barged into Tom's office. "Bartlett!" he yelled. "You incompetent boob! I just saw Valderon! What's the big plan, now that you have no chef for the opening?" Jonathan noticed Amanda standing there. "Oh, excuse me," he said politely.

"I was just leaving," Amanda answered coldly.

Lois put her arm around Amanda's shoulder. "Jonathan, this is Amanda Shelton. She made *the éclairs*," she said, hoping Jonathan would jump to a solution to their problem.

Jonathan grinned, remembering the sensations the little pastries had delivered. "Oh. Oh! *Oh!*" he said, and turned to Tom. "Bartlett! You're a genius! First you get rid of that French twit and then you get this heavenly creature to cook for my restaurant! *Brilliant!* Cutting it a little close, but I admire that kind of ruthless risk-taking!"

It dawned on Amanda what had just occurred. This man was Tom's boss, and he assumed she was there to replace Valderon. What a laugh! Not only was it way beyond her to cook for so many people, she wouldn't do it for Tom. Not after he'd made known his feelings—or *lack* of feelings—for her. "I'm not cooking for him!" she said defiantly.

"No," Tom agreed, "she's not cooking for me."

"Why not?" Jonathan asked. "Do you only do desserts?"

"No, but—"

"Is everything else as good as those incredible pastries?" he asked.

"Yes, I think so," Amanda said. "But—"

Lois jumped in to seal the deal. "Tom was just saying what a magical chef Amanda is."

Tom turned on Lois. "*Magical*? I'd say demonic is more like it. Besides, she *can't* do it, Jonathan. She doesn't have the experience."

That was all Amanda needed to hear: *She can't do it.* How dare he? Now she'd *have* to do it just to prove him wrong, just to prove she *could*. She smiled a tight smile and looked at Jonathan. "Oh, but Tom's wrong. Of course I can do it. I have years of experience. Didn't you see the review in today's *Times*?"

Tom blanched. "You can't be serious! Amanda, this is a huge job. You think you can replace a four-star chef with twenty-three years of experience?"

Amanda gave him a withering look. "I'm magical. You said so yourself."

Jonathan frowned at Tom, then turned to Amanda. "Can you do this job tomorrow?"

"Yes," she said confidently.

"No," Tom countered.

"It's settled, then," Jonathan said. "She's doing it."

Tom fell back into his chair, his head in his hands.

Jonathan touched Lois's elbow. "Do you mind showing Amanda the kitchen while I have a word with Tom?" Then he whispered in Lois's ear, "Are you busy after I'm done chewing Tom's head off?"

"Of course," Lois replied. She offered him a small smile, then turned and steered Amanda out the door.

Jonathan launched into Tom. "My god, Bartlett, you're not the man I hired. What the hell has gotten into you?"

Tom leaned forward, eyes ablaze. "*She* did! She's some kind of witch, Jonathan, you don't know what she can do—"

Jonathan looked annoyed. "I'm not interested in your sick private life. She's a great cook, and she's available tomorrow night when a hundred people are expecting to be served the most incredible food in the world—"

"Let me try to get Valderon back," Tom pleaded.

"You blew that one," Jonathan said. "You talked me into this restaurant business. Now you'd better find the nerve to follow through. Now's not the time to be choking, Bartlett."

Tom tried to explain. "She could destroy us, you don't understand—"

Jonathan had had enough of Tom's whining. He'd never seen him so rattled. "She's cooking. Develop some courage." He turned to go, then added before storming out, "And shave while you're at it. You look a mess."

Meanwhile, Lois showed Amanda the kitchen. Some of Valderon's sous-chefs were still working, but others had decided to leave out of loyalty to him. Amanda eyed the awesome, gleaming room filled with state-of-the-art appliances. Pots, pans, and utensils lined the counters and walls. It was about five times the size of her kitchen.

"You should find everything you need," Lois said. "Tom wanted the kitchen to be top-of-the-line."

Amanda was speechless, her mouth nearly hanging open. A sous-chef with devious little eyes sized her up and then smirked. "My name is François," he said, holding out his hand.

Amanda instinctively distrusted his gesture of friendship, but she shook his hand out of politeness. "Nice to meet you," she said.

Lois led Amanda from the kitchen to the hallway. "We'll see who of Valderon's team wants to stay. I assume you have your own assistants you'd like to bring up with you?"

Amanda thought of her "assistants"—Nolan, Stella, and Youssef—and tried to picture them in this fancy place. They were going to flip when they found out what she'd just signed them up for. "Yes, I do. Just a few, though, so I'd appreciate some of Valderon's too."

The two women walked down the hallway to the elevators, discussing the menu and other details. Lois wasn't sure, but she assumed Amanda would follow Valderon's recipes, since the menus were already printed. "I'll call you in a while to see how you're doing." She handed Amanda her card and shook her hand. Amanda didn't let go of Lois's hand. Lois smiled. "If you need anything, call me, even though I don't know how to do anything besides buy clothes."

"You know," Amanda said in a hushed and confidential tone, "I can't *really* do this."

"Of course you can. I read the review in the paper too. What is there to be afraid of?"

"That I've just been lucky for a few weeks. That it's not me—"

"It's just the beginning of a long lucky streak for you," Lois said, trying to reassure her. "But you'll need both hands, and so will I. Could you let go of mine now?"

Amanda realized she hadn't stopped shaking Lois's hand, and released it. "Sorry," she said. She stepped into the elevator.

"See you tomorrow," Lois said cheerfully. She couldn't wait to taste that food again.

"Yep!" Amanda said, trying to sound confident. The elevator dropped and so did her stomach. What had she gotten herself into?

Thirteen

Tom sat in the dark, empty restaurant and imagined how it would look in less than twenty-four hours: Well-dressed people would be eating—*what?* What would Amanda cook? He went over the events of the past weeks and tried to make sense of them. He'd never made such a mess of things so fast. The chef he'd worked so hard to land had walked out the day before the opening. His boss was on his case for screwing up. And the girl he *knew* he loved didn't know it because he was too afraid to let himself fall in love. And so he had blown it with her too. To think she was a witch—only a fool would think that and not see that everything that had happened, had happened because of the magic between them. Even the floating—why couldn't he have just gone with it and had fun?

But now it was too late. If he told her how he really felt, she'd think he was just saying it so that she'd do a good job on the restaurant's opening night. But if he *didn't* tell her, and she was as mad as she seemed, she could cook something terrible and ruin him. He wished he could see her, talk to her for just a minute. And then the door opened and she walked in.

"Oh—what are you doing here?" She was shocked to see Tom sitting alone in the dark restaurant. "Dumb question," she answered herself. "You work here. You're probably wondering what *I'm* doing here." Nervously she rattled on. "Well, I wanted to get a feel for the place and do some prep tonight so that tomorrow—"

"I understand," he said, happy to see her.

"You do?" she asked.

He nodded. "Sure. Do you have everything you need?"

"I wouldn't mind a little more confidence, but besides that—"

"You'll be great," he said, meaning it.

"You think so?" she asked.

Tom paused, wanting to take her in his arms but afraid again. "I know so."

Amanda scanned the large restaurant. "Well,

me too, then. I mean, if you're not worried, I'm not worried." She knew she was trying to convince herself. "Because what's to worry about? I can cook Valderon's recipes for one hundred people in just under two hours, no problem, right? I mean, with his staff to help me, and a little luck, everything will be just fine."

Tom searched Amanda's face, gripping the back of a chair. "You wouldn't do anything . . . what I mean is, I hope you won't do anything funny tomorrow. You know, like make the food make people do weird things."

"Like float?" Amanda asked.

"Or throw plates, or—"

"Don't worry," Amanda said reassuringly. "I promise I'll just cook and nothing weird will happen."

"Great, great," Tom said. "Well, I'd better get going," He suddenly felt reluctant to leave her.

"Yeah, me too. Big day tomorrow." Amanda looked at him shyly, unable to read his expression. Did he still care?

"See you soon," he said, and walked out.

Amanda went into the kitchen and hoped

she'd be able to live up to her promise. She didn't know why weird things happened when she cooked. She could only do her best and hope that somehow her feelings wouldn't flow into the food. She started rolling out pastry dough for the peach pockets she planned to make for dessert. It wasn't on Valderon's menu, but she knew no one would be disappointed. When the vanilla-orchid fog puffed out of each little pocket, she was sure the diners would be more than delighted.

Fourteen

Stella slammed a big stack of money on the bar. It was early, but Nolan and Youssef were already there, ready to go uptown, along with Stella, to help Amanda prepare for her big night. "You guys look like you could use one of my super-duper triple-back-flip espressos," Stella said.

"I'm not a morning person," Youssef apologized. "Espresso might help me become one."

"That's a nice chunk of change," Nolan said about the stack of bills. "Rent money?"

"Yep. I think we made it," Stella said as she slid the espressos across the bar. "I guess it's true what they say, it's not over till it's over."

Amanda walked in.

"Espresso, honey?" Stella asked.

"A triple back flip, please. I was up too late folding pastry into little envelopes."

"That's not on the menu," Nolan said.

"I know, but I have to have a little fun, don't I?" Amanda noticed the stack of cash. "Did we make it, Aunt Stella?"

"Just about. Would you mind counting it to be sure? I have to drop it off this morning or we're out of here. You know what a butthead that landlord is."

Amanda counted the worn bills. In a few minutes she'd counted four thousand dollars. "I think we should start taking credit cards," she said. She felt proud and knew her mother would have been proud too. Amanda's dream had finally come true; thanks to her secret recipes, the Southern Cross would go on operating. "Four thousand, nine hundred and ninety-six . . . ninety-seven, ninety-eight, ninety-nine—Oh, no!"

"Give me a break," Stella said, incredulous.

"Wait, I think I've got it," Amanda said. She dug into her pocket and slapped a coin on the counter. It was a silver dollar—the same silver dollar she'd tossed off the bridge that day, the same silver dollar that the strange little crab man had given back to her at the market. "Five thousand!" she said with a laugh.

Stella kissed her. "You earned every dollar of this, my dear. And no one's prouder of you than your old aunt."

The four of them finished their coffees and headed out. Nolan and Youssef had never been to Bendel's, and as they entered the grand lobby they felt intimidated.

"I suppose the restaurant has a similar, completely-out-of-my-league kind of feel to it?" Nolan asked weakly.

"Relax, it's only a department store," Amanda said, pleased that she was now comfortable enough to reassure her friend.

"*Some* department store," Youssef said, obviously impressed with every square inch of the beautiful place. "I can't wait to see the restaurant."

When they walked into Jonathan's, Amanda started to feel nervous again. Waiters were setting up beautiful tables; florists were filling huge vases with their arrangements. The patrons would be expecting equally extravagant food.

Instinctively Amanda reached up to rub her lucky earrings—but they weren't there.

"My earrings!" she cried, terrified.

"You look fine," Nolan said, standing in the doorway of the kitchen. "Wow. . . . Look at this place."

Amanda tugged at her ears in disbelief. "No, no. . . . This all started happening when I put on my mom's earrings."

Nolan looked at Amanda as if she was nuts. "You think they're magic?"

"Why else did my cooking suddenly get so good?" she asked.

Nolan realized she was serious. He had to set her straight. "Because that day, when Tom walked in, you wanted to be good—*really* good. And you wanted it bad enough. That's the magic. Not those old earrings. They're not even that cool."

"Nolan . . . ," Amanda whined.

"Hey, even Dumbo could fly without his feather, right? Now, come on, introduce us to these dudes," he said. The kitchen was a beehive of Frenchmen in white.

"Excuse me!" Amanda said, trying to sound authoritative. It didn't work. No one seemed to even notice she was there. She would have to be more aggressive. She put her fingers to her lips and let go with the whistle that she used to hail a taxi. Everyone turned and stared at her.

She faced the kitchen crew. "I—I—I just wanted to say . . . *hello*!" She waved, feeling like a moron. "I'm Amanda Shelton, the, um, chef," she added with a nervous laugh. "And this is Nolan Traynor, my chief sous-chef. And . . . I'm sure you all know exactly what you're doing. Thank you . . . and carry on."

The Frenchmen immediately returned to their work.

Amanda took a deep breath and nodded. "See? We're off to a great start here." She pulled the little crab from her bag—maybe *he* was her lucky charm? *Like a witch's familiar, only instead of a cat it's a crab*, she thought. She set the crab on a high counter and filled a plate with water for him. "Stay close," she whispered. "I'm going to need all the friends I can get."

"Excuse me, *mademoiselle*," said a French voice, dripping with false friendliness. "Remember me? I am François de Maigre. The right hand of Monsieur Valderon. If you like, I have a suggestion."

"Wonderful!" Amanda said. Maybe she'd judged him wrong; maybe he hadn't been sneering at her the day before.

"I have worked for the greatest chef in the world for fifteen years. I offer to carry on in his behalf, and you may stay and watch—"

"That's very kind, François, but I really couldn't do that. You see, Mr. Bendel asked me to cook tonight. You understand," Amanda said, trying to sound as condescending as François did.

"I see," he said huffily. "In that case, what would you like?"

"Well, maybe you could do what you normally do."

"Of course." François didn't move. He stood still, staring at Amanda.

"Okay, so let's get started," she said, hoping he'd disappear and go chop things, or whatever he did, somewhere else.

"I have, *mademoiselle*," he said arrogantly.

"What are you doing?"

"Waiting. For *instructions*. Monsieur Valderon always gives instructions."

Amanda pursed her lips, "*Right*. Okay. Hmmm . . . um, hors d'oeuvres."

"Completed!" François said proudly, a self-satisfied smile spreading across his face. He leaned against the counter, then jumped. *"Aggggh!"* The crab had pinched him. Panicked, François tried to shake him off. Amanda laughed, gently removing the crab. He scampered under a refrigerator.

"The little beast!" François whimpered, storming off.

Amanda was feeling better already.

Lois was dressed in a silvery satin gown with crystal beads accenting the bodice. She felt more beautiful than she could ever remember feeling. She was full of anticipation; if just a few éclairs could make her and Jonathan feel the way they had, what might happen tonight, with a three-course meal?

She scanned the grand dining room, looking for Tom, who she knew was probably in a panic. Waiters were putting the final touches on the tables: silver candlesticks and vases with white roses. The band was setting up on the stage. Everything was nearly ready.

She hurried out of the restaurant and went to the executive offices, finding Tom just leaving his office in his tuxedo—but with no pants on.

"Tom?" Lois said gently.

"Oh, hi, Lois." He was very distracted. Obviously.

She took his arm, turning him around. "Wait, wait, let's go back to your office for a sec."

"Why?" he asked irritably.

"Because you forgot to put your pants on," Lois hissed.

Tom looked down and saw for himself. "My god!" he said, jumping. "What's the matter with me?"

"Nothing a pair of tuxedo pants won't fix," she replied casually.

He found the pants in his closet and slipped them on, muttering all the time. "This is going to be a disaster, Lois. I've been thinking about it. She can't help but tamper with the food, so our only hope is to get Jonathan to realize it, and then we'll let Valderon's chief assistant take over—"

"Shut up, Tom, you're babbling and making absolutely no sense," Lois said. Taking him by the shoulders, she stared into his face. "Everything will be fine. It's only a dinner, for god's sake. You'd think you were going before the firing squad."

Tom looked out his window to Fifth Avenue below. Streams of limousines and taxis were pulling up to Bendel's entrance for the opening. "That's what it feels like," he mumbled, and he left his office to greet the guests.

Tom and Lois stood on the landing of the sweeping central staircase and watched the first diners arrive. The party had become the most sought-after invitation in New York. There were media moguls and models, movie stars and millionaires, fashion designers and food critics— and, of course, the paparazzi were there, flashing their cameras at everyone. All the TV stations were covering the glamorous event. Tom and Lois greeted each guest with a handshake or an air kiss.

Jonathan joined them, sliding an arm around Lois's waist and kissing her neck. "You look good enough to eat!" he said. "Stupendously spectacular, Lois!"

"Thank you, Jonathan." She beamed.

"You, on the other hand," Jonathan said, looking Tom over, "look a little pale."

Lois jumped in. "He's just so excited, all the blood has left his head."

A huge man and woman lumbered up the steps. Jonathan recognized them and introduced them to Lois and Tom. "Frank Rogers and Hannah Wallberg of *The New York Times*. This is Lois McNally, my fashion director, and Tom Bartlett, general manager of the store." They all nodded at each other.

Frank Rogers spoke. "Very brave of you, inviting us for opening night. I suppose with Valderon in the kitchen, there's nothing to worry about. Stroke of genius getting him, Bendel."

"Yes, yes, thank you," Jonathan said. After the critics had moved on, Jonathan took Tom aside. "Let's see how your chef is doing, Bartlett."

"*My* chef?" But Tom knew there was no sense in arguing with Jonathan; Jonathan was the boss. Tom slowly followed him up the stairs and toward the kitchen, afraid of what they would find there.

Amanda stood in the kitchen in dismay, having just discovered that a key ingredient was missing. Her hair was dusted white with flour, her apron smeared with many colorful sauces. She put her hands on her hips and shouted, *"What are you talking about? No truffles?"*

François was totally calm. "*Oui.* Not a one. Monsieur Valderon brought them from France himself, so naturally, he took them back to France when he departed."

At this very inopportune moment, and unknown to Amanda, Jonathan and Tom entered the kitchen.

"I can't make truffle slippers without truffles!" she cried.

"But could you make them *with* truffles?" François asked scornfully.

"François, everything okay in here?" Tom said, worried by the sight of a crazed Amanda. She whipped around, horrified to find him there. How much had he heard?

"Everything is fine," she replied. "Super, in fact," she added cheerily. She glared at François for confirmation.

"Nous nageons dans une mer des ordures," he said with his supercilious smile.

Neither Jonathan nor Tom understood French, which was good, because François had said, "We are swimming in a sea of garbage." But the impression Jonathan got was that everything was okay, so he left the kitchen.

Tom paused, wanted to say something to Amanda, but he felt awkward with everyone around. He looked at her helplessly, shrugged, and walked out.

Amanda hurled the spoon she was holding at the door and stormed over to the counter. Tears sparkled in her eyes, she was so frustrated and nervous and mad. *Why couldn't he have said something? Why?* As she stirred the sauce, the tears fell, dropping into the bubbling brew. He could have winked or smiled at her! And what was she going to make without the truffles? It was the main ingredient of the first dish! More tears spilled into the sauce. The mixture changed color with each tear that fell, but Amanda didn't notice.

"Amanda?" Nolan stood holding a tray of tiny slippers made out of pastry. The truffles were meant to fill them, drizzled with the sauce she was stirring. Now the slippers would be empty and would taste like . . . sawdust. The appetizer would be a disaster. Nolan saw his friend's tears and tried to cheer her up. He said quietly, so that only she would hear: "It's the NBA championship, there's five seconds left, your team's behind by a point. They bring the ball up, you're cross-court, they hit you coming across the key, you're at the net, there's only two seconds left now, you're there, the net's in your face and you . . ."

Amanda looked at her friend and wondered what in the world he was talking about. Maybe he'd lost it too.

"Do you really call time out for a good cry?" He looked at her, but still she wasn't following him. "*Noooo!* You *shoot*, Amanda! *Now, shoot!*"

"Ohhhh," she said, finally getting it. "This is one of those stupid sports analogies, isn't it?"

"Yeah, but as long as you get it it's not stupid."

Amanda took a deep breath and collected herself. "Okay. I got it." She had to rally. Nolan was right. She couldn't give up at the first sign of trouble. There was no time to run out and buy truffles, so she'd just have to use her imagination. There must be something in the kitchen that she could use instead. Something that would go with the sauce and the pastry, which were already prepared. She looked over Valderon's menu and got an idea.

She yelled at François—in French. "Hey, you, who thinks I don't speak French! Give me those figs!"

François turned red when he realized Amanda had understood every nasty word he'd said. "The figs? But they are for the dessert."

The little crab had scurried out from behind the refrigerator as if to cheer her on. "I'll just have to do a little rearranging is all," she told the crab with renewed resolve. "The menu just changed."

Tom was pacing. Where were the appetizers? He looked at his watch: 8:14. He'd assumed they would be serving by now. The guests must be getting hungry. He looked at his watch again: 8:15. What if she was in there but not cooking at all? What if they were all waiting for—*nothing*?

"Loosen up, Bartlett, do your job," Jonathan said as he brushed past, smiling at the German department store executives. Just then waiters started coming through the kitchen doors with silver trays held high over their shoulders.

"Here we go," Tom said with relief, and took his seat.

Frank Rogers and Hannah Wallberg, the food critics, were already at their table, waiting with great anticipation. Valderon was their hero, a chef of the old school who had a magic touch that could transform even a roast chicken into a one-of-a-kind gastronomical event. They had requested a table for six for themselves, claiming they needed privacy to be fair, but really, they wanted the additional space because they intended to take two or three helpings of each dish.

"Ah, the truffle slipper!" Hannah sighed as a beautiful, delicate pastry slipper resting on a golden sauce was placed in front of her. This was one of Valderon's most celebrated inventions. "Please, leave a few more of those," she said, grabbing the waiter before he could leave. "We need to check for consistency in the cooking, you understand."

Frank and Hannah raised their forks in unison. Tom watched them from his table. They cut into the slippers and took a bite, both of them rolling the hors d'oeuvre around in their mouths as if it was a fine wine. They swallowed. They waited. Then, together, they declared: "Exceptional!"

Frank added, "The fig is an inspired choice."

Hannah remarked, "Valderon's new interpretation of his signature dish. Like a delightful variation on a theme."

"I can see this night may be full of unexpected pleasures," Frank said.

From a few tables away, Tom observed that the critics seemed to be enjoying the appetizer. They were eating a second helping already—surely that was a good sign.

"Tom, try this. It's fabulous," Lois said, but he was too nervous to eat. He got up to walk the room, and to his horror discovered that the guests who had finished their food were—*crying*! A tableful of models was weeping, the mayor and the news anchor were sobbing—even the Germans were wiping their eyes! What was going on? Tom overheard snippets of their conversations.

"Binky, my Binky," Mr. Mueller, the chairman of the German department store, sobbed.

"Oh, my little schnitzel, who's Binky?" his wife asked through her own tears.

"My cat! My poor, poor kitty . . ."

"But my darling, you don't have a cat."

"She died! When I was ten!" They hugged each other, as many other guests around the room were doing.

When he saw that Frank and Hannah were crying too, Tom panicked.

Frank sobbed, "Hannah, this is sensational. The foie gras melts in your mouth. If only I could cook like this. I so wanted to be a chef!"

"I never knew that. Me too!" she confessed. "They rejected me at the Cordon Bleu!"

"Me too! Oh, Hannah . . . ," he cried.

Tom rushed back to Jonathan's table, while Stella, who had also noticed all the upset, high-tailed it into the kitchen.

"Amanda! Amanda, stop! Where is she?" Stella moved around the army of waiters, who were bringing in the empty appetizer plates and loading up with the entree, risotto cakes and smoked duck breast.

"What's going on, Stella?" Nolan asked.

"She did something to the food—everyone's crying!" Stella exclaimed.

Amanda came out of the walk-in refrigerator

and saw the horror on Stella's face. Stella nodded for Amanda to look out at the dining room.

"Don't panic. Promise me you'll remain calm," Stella said.

Amanda, Stella, and Nolan stood just inside the dining room and stared as each tableful of guests wept, sobbed, cried, and sighed. Amanda saw Tom arguing with Jonathan. That was all she needed to see to let out a cry herself and run back into the kitchen.

"You said you'd stay calm," Stella said as she and Nolan followed.

Meanwhile, Tom was trying to control the damage. He'd known Amanda would pull something—but *crying*! What a disaster!

"No, it's fantastic!" Jonathan said. "The food's delicious, and everybody loves a good cry now and then. It's like great group therapy! Look around—everybody's refreshed. Nobody's complaining, Tom, except you," Jonathan added, a few tears still falling down his cheek.

Lois dabbed her eyes and put an arm around Jonathan. "It's so good to see you letting it all out, Jonathan. I knew there was a sensitive man inside that tough, rock-hard physique." They kissed and dried each other's tears.

Tom felt as if he was on another planet. He slowly made his way back to his seat, hoping Jonathan was right.

Meanwhile, Amanda was having a panic attack, even though Stella kept saying, "Don't have a panic attack."

"No?" Amanda asked. "You don't think making a hundred people cry is a reason to have a panic attack?"

What could Stella say?

Then Nolan spoke up. "Hey, but no one's leaving."

"So?" Amanda said.

He explained, "It means they're not _upset_ about crying. If they were, we'd know. The food must be too good, Amanda. They want more. So you gotta keep going. Just try to keep your tears out of the food this time."

Stella looked at the last trays of entrees leaving the kitchen. "How were you feeling when you made those?" She hated to ask, but she wanted to be prepared.

"Fine," Amanda replied. "I was determined to just do a great job with them."

"Well then, I'm sure there's nothing to worry about," Stella said, and they both peeked out into the dining room.

The guests cut into the duck and risotto. Soon the dining room was absolutely silent. Even the band stopped playing, as if out of respect. François pushed through the swinging doors into the kitchen.

"*Mademoiselle?* I assume you are leaving now that you have shocked them into silence!"

Amanda had had enough of this guy. She ignored him and went out into the dining room to see for herself. Nolan and Stella followed. The three stood at the edge of the quiet room. The only sound was the clinking of forks against china.

Nolan spoke in a hushed tone, "Uh-oh. We'd better get out of here. I think there's a midnight flight to New Guinea. They'll never find us there. You know any recipes for ox, Amanda?"

"Shhh," she said, listening to the silence.

"This is amazing. This is the best it can be," she said, not quite believing it herself.

"It's like they're in a trance," Stella observed.

"Does that mean we can make them do anything we want?" Nolan asked.

"Not us," Stella said, "but *she* could."

"Excellent!" Nolan said to Amanda. "Make all the pretty girls love me and the rich men give me their wallets."

And then something in Amanda's head clicked. It was time to stop being passive about her talent, whatever it was exactly. She could stop letting it control her and let herself control it.

This much she knew: When she cooked with all her love, the food made people feel wonderful. And if she couldn't make Tom feel wonderful enough to come into the kitchen and take her in his arms, then he simply didn't love her, and she would give up on him.

"Nolan," she said, "I can't control people like that, but I might be able to do something else." She turned to go back into the kitchen, pushing one swinging door open just as François was

coming out. The door clunked him on the forehead, and Amanda stifled a smile.

François collected himself and said, "*Voilà!*
So now that you have ruined this night, you can
take your little bag back to your little restaurant
where *little* cooks belong. I will proceed with the
dessert, a lovely recipe of my own, made with
rum raisin *crème*—"

"*Rum raisin?*" Amanda looked at Nolan.
"He *would* like rum raisin." She took her place
at the counter. "François, you're such a disappointment. Why don't you take the rest of the
night off?"

Out of François's sight, Nolan gave Amanda
a thumbs-up. "You go, girl," he said. François
stormed off, and Amanda, now clearly in control, started organizing the dessert. "In the
walk-in there are trays of peach pockets and
some bunches of orchids. I need the heavy
cream, some sugar . . ." Nolan and the others
leapt into action, and the kitchen was abustle
again.

Meanwhile, out in the dining room, Tom was
at his wits' end. The place had gone so quiet,

they might have been in a church. He ran to Jonathan. "Jonathan, I think it's time I get the sous-chef to take over. Maybe we can salvage the dessert—"

"Bartlett, you're an idiot. Did you try this?" Jonathan asked.

"Why is it so quiet?" Tom asked.

"Shhh!" Lois said, bringing a fork to his lips. "Isn't it nutty?"

"Yes, yes, crazy—" Tom began.

"No, *hazel*-nutty!" Lois declared.

And then Lois practically swooned against Jonathan and fed him the duck. Once again, Tom felt as if he was really out of it. He decided it was time to go. He probably was fired, anyway. In the morning, when Jonathan was no longer under the influence of Amanda's cooking, he would read all about it in the papers and realize what a fiasco the night had been.

Tom took the elevator upstairs to his office. A janitor was there, adjusting the wings on one of the paper airplanes. "Hey! What are you do-ing! Don't touch that!"

The janitor was none other than Gene

O'Reilly, the man who'd sold Amanda the special crabs. "Your wings looked a little rigid, Tom," he said with a smile. "You need to relax them. That way you can catch unexpected updrafts and go unexpected places."

Tom listened carefully to what the strange little man said. It seemed to make sense, and yet it was such simple advice, why had he never figured it out himself?

"Think about it," Gene said. "It applies to more than paper airplanes." And then he emptied the wastebasket into a big bag and left Tom's office. It wasn't until he had gone that Tom realized Gene had called him by his name, as if he knew him. *He must have seen my letterhead*, Tom assured himself, and slid the paper airplane into this pocket. He looked out the window at Fifth Avenue, and at the full moon overhead. The city looked beautiful, and he wished Amanda could be with him at that moment.

He was surprised to feel that way. After all his resistance, he had to admit, he wanted her. And it was time to listen to his heart—not his head, or his fears, or his stupid ideas of how to keep things in control. He was tired of fighting his desire for her—and he couldn't understand why he ever had. After seeing an entire roomful of strangers succumb to the magic that was Amanda, he knew only a fool wouldn't want to be a part of it. If he was lucky, he'd still have a chance to tell her that he didn't want to be a fool anymore.

Dessert was served. As the guests cut into the peach pockets, a silvery white sauce oozed out and an enchanting puff of vanilla fog escaped. The fog drifted over the plates and rolled across the tables, encircling lovers' hands and tickling their legs as it blanketed the floor. The band started playing "That Old Black Magic," and couples made their way to the dance floor.

Jonathan and Lois started dancing. Without realizing it, they slowly floated off the ground just a few inches, actually dancing on a cloud.

Tom had returned to the dining room to find it full of the vanilla fog, the dance floor crowded with happy couples. Even the food critics were embracing at their table, feeding each other third and fourth helpings of Amanda's amazing dessert.

Tom was stunned by the sight of the glittering room. He knew how wonderful everyone in it was feeling. He also recognized that Amanda was sending him a message by preparing that romantic dish for this important night. She was saying, *Look. If all these people like the feeling, why can't you?*

He dashed into the kitchen. The little crab scuttled across the floor and grabbed his pants cuff. "You again?" Tom asked. "Where's Amanda?" The crab let go and ran back under the counter.

Nolan and Stella were helping the other sous-chefs with the cleanup. "She left," Nolan said.

"Left? Why?" Tom asked.

Stella looked at him angrily. "*Now* you come into the kitchen? After this whole long night, *now* you come in to see her?" Stella couldn't help being fed up with any guy who would treat her niece like this.

Nolan nudged Stella, wanting her to cool it. "She was finished, so she left," he told Tom.

Tom was crestfallen.

Nolan went on, "She *just* left, man. You still might be able to catch her."

That was all Tom needed to hear. He ran for the elevators and hit the button about a hundred times. Finally an elevator came. He rode down to he ground floor, rushed through the store, and burst out onto the street. He frantically looked both ways but couldn't see her. Dejected, he rushed back into the store and stepped into the elevator, pushing the button for his office floor.

Amanda hadn't yet left the store. After walking out of the restaurant, she had decided to take the grand staircase down through the center of the store, wanting to savor her last minutes there. The store felt like a palace to her, and her time there had been like a dream that was near its end. As she walked through the glamorous lobby, she felt no bitterness, only sadness. She knew that even though Tom didn't love her, she had fallen in love with him and would miss him very much.

Tom was so depressed, he couldn't face the party again. He sat in the window of his office and looked out at Fifth Avenue. It was late, so the avenue was not crowded. He opened the window to get some air, leaning his head out a bit. And then he saw her. Amanda stood opposite the store, waiting for a taxi.

"Amanda! Amanda!" he shouted. She didn't hear him. She lifted her fingers to her lips and whistled. A taxi pulled over to the curb.

Tom panicked. There was no time to race down eight flights of steps—by then she'd be gone. He had to talk to her and be with her— tonight—*now*. And then it occurred to him. It was crazy, but it was his only chance. He took from his pocket the paper airplane that the old janitor had adjusted and gave its wings a tweak.

"Don't fail me now," he said. He blew on it for extra luck. And then he shot it out the window, watching as it gracefully sailed down, down, down, across the street and over the traffic, until it slid quickly into the open window of the taxi.

Amanda had just arranged herself in the backseat when the paper airplane flew inside and landed in her lap. She looked at the plane, knowing it could have come from only one person. When she leaned out the window, she saw Tom waving to her from his office.

"Now, *that* is incredible," she whispered to herself. "Wait," she told the driver. She stepped from the cab and hurried across the street to the store, thrilled that Tom wanted to see her enough to make his own magic happen.

She waited at the elevator bank a long time. Just when she was about to take the stairs, the doors opened.

Inside the elevator, a mannequin stood wearing the beautiful pink satin gown Amanda had admired that first day at Bendel's. A little note was pinned to the mannequin. It said AMANDA, WEAR ME.

The minute Tom saw Amanda get out of the

cab, he ran to Evening Wear, lifted the mannequin right off the stand, and set it in the elevator. And now he waited and waited for Amanda
to walk off the elevator wearing the gown. The
elevator stopped on the third floor. *I guess she's
changing*, he thought, about to burst with impa-
tience. Finally the elevator doors *ping*ed open—
but Amanda wasn't there. Instead he saw the
now unclothed mannequin, with a new note.
This one read THANKS!

He couldn't believe it. Had she taken the
dress and left? She couldn't have.

"Hey there," a voice said behind him.

Tom whipped around to see Amanda in the
gown, looking more beautiful than he could
have dreamed.

He sighed. "Are you trying to kill me?" he
laughed.

Amanda lifted a foot and tilted her ankle. "I
had to stop for shoes."

"You are so beautiful. . . ." He kissed her,
hoping it would express everything he felt. "I'm
sorry I've been so stupid. I was scared, and an idiot for not following my heart. I guess I didn't

know how to do it. But there's one thing I do know: I want you, Amanda. Give me another chance?"

Tears rose in her eyes, she was so moved and happy. "You're so dense, you might need a third or fourth," she said, making him laugh again.

"Okay, okay, I'll take as many as you'll give me." He took her hand and led her to the dining room. He noticed that she held the paper airplane in her other hand.

"Pretty amazing aerodynamic phenomenon, don't you think?" he said jokingly. There was no more denying it: magical, amazing things could happen, if you'd just let them. He didn't need to understand how *everything* worked. He could relax his wings a little. Amanda had taught him that.

The dance floor was full, the sweet vanilla fog still working its magic on the guests. "Wait right here," Tom said. He ran up to the band as it finished a song. He stood at the microphone and addressed the crowd. A spotlight shone on him.

"I have a confession to make," he said. "First

of all, Valderon did not cook tonight's incredible meal."

There was a loud *"Ooooh"* from the guests.

"And second of all, I'm in love with the amazing woman who did. It's my honor and privilege to introduce you to an extraordinary chef and the most beautiful woman in the world, Amanda Shelton." The spotlight found her, and the crowd parted, applauding. Amanda felt embarrassed—but also very, very happy.

As Tom walked through the crowd toward Amanda, Jonathan pulled him aside. "Glad to see you've come to your senses, Bartlett."

Lois added, "Literally!"

The band began playing "Bewitched, Bothered, and Bewildered." Tom joined Amanda.

Stella wept, she was so moved and proud as she watched Tom take Amanda onto the dance floor. Someone tapped her shoulder. "Care to dance?" the gentleman asked. Stella smiled and said yes.

The man seemed familiar, but she couldn't place him at first. And then she remembered. "Hey, aren't you Gene O'Reilly?" she said.

Gene smiled. "That I am," he said.

"But wait, aren't you . . . *dead*?" Stella whispered.

"I may be old, but I'm certainly not *that* old," he said with a smile. "Are you insulting my dancing, *madame*?" He whisked her across the floor.

Stella decided not to push it. The way things had been going lately, there seemed no sense in trying to figure everything out. She should simply enjoy whatever the world was offering. He was a good dancer, so why bother with the details?

Tom couldn't take his eyes off Amanda. "I love you," he said. And then he said it again, just because he felt it so strongly.

Amanda's heart jumped. She looked into his eyes and suddenly felt afraid. What if it was only the mood her dessert had given him? "I hope it's not just the fog talking."

He laughed. "It's not. I didn't eat a thing all night!"

Amanda laughed in return. "Good . . . 'cause I really love you."

"I think I've loved you since that day in the market," he said.

"You mean when I had my hand up your pants?" She grinned. "Men are so easy."

Tom twirled her around the dance floor, then held her close. And slowly, slowly, they started floating. They floated higher and higher as the band played on and the other couples watched them in wonder. Although it was an amazing sight, no one seemed alarmed, because after all, in New York, anything can happen.